A Forever Kind of

Love

A Forever Kind of

Love

Vanessa

Miller

Book 3
Praise Him Anyhow Series

Vanessa Miller
www.vanessamiller.com

Printed in the United States of America
© 2013 by Vanessa Miller

Praise Unlimited Enterprises
Charlotte, NC

Other Books by Vanessa Miller

How Sweet The Sound
Heirs of Rebellion
The Best of All
Better for Us
Her Good Thing
Long Time Coming
A Promise of Forever Love
A Love for Tomorrow
Yesterday's Promise
Forgotten
Forgiven
Forsaken
Rain for Christmas (Novella)
Through the Storm
Rain Storm
Latter Rain
Abundant Rain
Former Rain

Anthologies (Editor)
Keeping the Faith
Have A Little Faith
This Far by Faith

EBOOKS

Love Isn't Enough

A Mighty Love

The Blessed One (Blessed and Highly Favored series)

The Wild One (Blessed and Highly Favored Series)

The Preacher's Choice (Blessed and Highly Favored Series)

The Politician's Wife (Blessed and Highly Favored Series)

The Playboy's Redemption (Blessed and Highly Favored Series)

Tears Fall at Night (Praise Him Anyhow Series)

Joy Comes in the Morning (Praise Him Anyhow Series)

A Forever Kind of Love (Praise Him Anyhow Series)

Ramsey's Praise (Praise Him Anyhow Series)

Escape to Love (Praise Him Anyhow Series)

Praise For Christmas (Praise Him Anyhow Series)

His Love Walk (Praise Him Anyhow Series)

Journals

Praise Him Anyhow Journal

Prologue

Looking like a GQ model in his black Armani suit and his yellow tie with tiny black dots, with dimples on both sides of his handsome face, Dontae Marshall put the two-carat Princess cut diamond ring in his pocket. Dontae would have gladly purchased a five-carat ring if need be, but the woman he had fallen in love with didn't hunger and thirst for displays of wealth as the first woman he'd fallen for had.

Dontae was so thankful that his sister, Joy had admonished him to pray about his decision to marry Tory Michaels. He hadn't appreciated the way Joy butted into his business at the time. But after he took that hit on the football field and then had to deal with rehabilitation for his knee, while worrying over his doctor's recommendation that he give up his football career, Dontae discovered that Tory was not the woman for him. She hadn't been in it for the right reasons.

Tory didn't love Dontae Marshall the man; she loved Dontae Marshall the football star. And the day he decided to follow doctor's orders and hang up his helmet, was the day that Tory started bringing him all kinds of drama. In the end, Dontae cut his losses by letting Tory keep that big rock he'd given her and then they both decided to go their separate ways. Soon after Dontae put his full concentration towards building the new career he had mapped out for himself.

It had taken a few years, but Dontae had used the money he'd received as a signing bonus to open a sports agency. Even though he couldn't play the game anymore, he still loved sports, so he sat down and had a talk with Stan Smith, his agent. Stan offered to take Dontae under his wing and he taught him the sports agency business and just like that, Dontae found a new purpose in life. He was passionate about protecting young athletes from some of the nonsense that went on behind the scenes. Dontae believed that his job was to help navigate his clients around a system designed to favor the owners—and sometimes even coaches—rather than the players.

After learning as much as he could from his mentor, Dontae relocated to Charlotte, North Carolina and set up shop. It didn't take long for his agency to gain a good name among the athletic community and his business grew right before his eyes. Dontae's mom had told him that his success was due to the fact that God had been watching out for him. Whether it was God's doing or something much simpler, Dontae didn't care, all he knew was that life was good.

Dontae hadn't imagined that things could get any better, but when he met Jewel Dawson, he realized that God had been holding out on him. Jewel was everything he wanted in a woman. She was soft spoken, yet in command at all times. Jewel was a writer who had taken her career into her own hands and was making a pretty good living. She was daring, loving, beautiful and most of all, she made him smile... no, not just smile, with Jewel, Dontae had learned to laugh and enjoy life again. He picked up the manila envelope, grabbed his keys and headed out the door.

***

Dontae took Jewel to Villa Antonio, her favorite Italian restaurant. The ambiance was perfect for a romantic dinner. Jewel was wearing a sleeveless silk dress that crisscrossed in the back. The dropped waistline on the dress gave way to a skirt designed for twirling movements. Dontae definitely approved. As a matter of fact, he couldn't take his eyes off of her.

"I love this place. I'm so glad you got us reservations here tonight," Jewel said as they were seated in a dimly lit corner of the restaurant.

"I know you love it, that's why we're here."

Jewel leaned over and kissed Dontae on his full, luscious lips. "Thanks baby, you're always thinking about me."

The couple ordered their food and then spent the evening gazing into each other's eyes. Dontae knew with everything in him that Jewel was the one for him. He was ready to make a life with her and didn't want to wait a moment longer. However, getting down on bended knee wasn't an option for him. Oh, he had recovered quite well from his knee injury several years back, but the knee would act up on him at times. And since this was an important moment—one that he wanted Jewel to remember for a lifetime—he didn't want to spoil it by needing the maître d's help when and if he failed to get up on his own.

Jewel's hands were resting on the table. Dontae laid his hands on top of hers, still gazing into his beloved's eyes he said, "Jewel, I want you to know that I am happy when I'm with you. You have brought so much joy into my life and, and—"

"Aw, that's so sweet," Jewel interrupted.

That's when Dontae remembered the ring that was in his jacket pocket. His hand shook with nervousness as he pulled it out and gripped it like he used to hold the football when charging his way to a touchdown. "I just believe that you and I are a perfect match. We fit together, ya' feel me?"

Jewel nodded. "I feel the same way, Dontae. I think I started falling in love with you the moment we met."

That revelation brought a smile to his face, gave him the strength to do what he had gone there to do. He was seated across from Jewel, but suddenly felt miles away. Dontae got up and squeezed in next to his woman. He set the ring box on the table and opened it.

Jewel gasped.

"What I'm trying to say is..."

Jewel wrapped her arms around Dontae and screamed, "Oh my God. Yes, yes, Dontae, I will marry you."

In a joking mood after receiving such a wonderful response to his almost proposal, he waited until she held out her hand for him to put the ring on her finger and then said, "You didn't let me finish my question. How do you know I was going to ask you to marry me? Maybe I just wanted to give you a ring to celebrate our one-year anniversary."

A hint of sadness dimmed Jewel's normally bright eyes. She quickly covered her face and said, "I'm so embarrassed. I should have let you finish. I'm sorry, Dontae."

He couldn't carry the joke any further. The look on Jewel's face told him that he'd gone too far. "No, I'm the one who is sorry. Of course I want to marry you. I was just joking, but I didn't mean to upset you."

Jewel shoved him. "Boy, you play too much."

"I'm sorry about that. But you already agreed to marry me, so you're stuck with me." He took the ring out of the box. "Can I put this on your finger and make it official?"

Grinning from ear to ear, Jewel held out her hand.

Dontae put the ring on her finger; they then celebrated with several kisses and Tiramisu. When they finished off their dessert, Dontae kissed his soon-to-be bride and then grabbed the manila envelope he'd left on the other side of the table and handed it to Jewel. "I almost forgot to give you this."

"What's this?" Jewel asked, while opening the envelope, still grinning at her man.

"Just a little document that I need you to sign and return to my attorney." He leaned back in his seat and added, "At your leisure, of course."

Jewel pulled the document out and read, then stared at it as if the words were written in Greek. After a long silent pause, she turned to him and asked, "Is this a joke?"

Dontae swiveled his head in order to take a glance at the paperwork in Jewel's hand. "No joke, babe, I just need you to sign those papers and return them to my attorney."

"Are you serious?"

"What's wrong?" Dontae asked, not understanding Jewel's reaction.

While shaking her head, Jewel told him, "This is turning out to be the worst proposal in the history of marriage proposals."

Confused by her reaction, Dontae said, "I thought I did good. I brought you to your favorite restaurant. I picked out a diamond that I knew you would love and then I... I —"

"And then you had the audacity to hand me a prenuptial agreement." Jewel threw the document down on the table and yanked the ring off her finger. "If you're so worried that the marriage won't last, I don't think we should even bother getting married in the first place."

Dontae had been leaning back, relaxing and enjoying the moment. But as he watched Jewel take the ring he'd just given her off her finger, a feeling of panic overtook him and he bolted into action. Holding up his hands trying to halt her tirade, Dontae said, "Hold up... you don't need to take that ring off. We're engaged now. I want to marry you."

Jewel put the ring in Dontae's hand and stood up. "Take me home."

"But baby."

"Take me home this instant, Dontae. I don't even want to talk to you right now."

"Baby, be reasonable. Don't you want to discuss the wedding?"

Jewel picked up the prenup, threw it in Dontae's face and then shoved his shoulders until he got up so that she could make her way out of the restaurant.

Dontae could see that he had lost the battle, so he did as Jewel asked so that he would have a shot at winning the war.

1

Carmella Marshall-Thomas was in the kitchen putting the finishing touches on the desserts she had made for Ramsey Jr's coming home party. Her husband's oldest son wasn't moving back to Raleigh as she and Ramsey had hoped, but he would be in Charlotte with Dontae and that was good enough for her. Carmella enjoyed throwing dinner parties for her family, so the Marshalls and Thomases were all gathering together again today.

Raven and Joy were in the kitchen helping her with the meal, while Renee hung out in the family room with Ramsey and Ronny. Dontae was driving in from Charlotte and had promised to pick up Ramsey Jr. from the airport on his way to the house. So as usual everyone would be there except for Ramsey's youngest son, the one with the heart of gold. Rashan was a missionary and had travelled all over the world during his short twenty-eight years of life, helping out and doing the Lord's work wherever needed.

"Okay ladies," Carmella addressed Joy, her natural born daughter and Raven her daughter from her marriage to Ramsey. Carmella and Ramsey had been married for eight years now, and Ramsey's children, the kids with the *R* names, didn't seem like step-children to her anymore. They were family and that's all Carmella had to say about that. "Looks like we have taken care of everything in here. Now all we have to do is set the table."

"Why don't we make Renee do that, since she didn't bother to help us fix one thing today," Raven demanded.

"I second that," Joy said. "Renee acts like she's allergic to pots and pans."

"You two need to leave your sister alone. She contributes to this family in other ways. But one day she will come to understand and appreciate the value of spending time with us in the kitchen," Carmella told her girls even as she prayed for that wish to come true. She so longed to be as close to Renee as she was with the rest of the children. But Carmella had learned the art of patience, so she was willing to wait until Renee felt comfortable enough to have a mother-daughter relationship with her.

"You're just too nice, Mom, that's all that is," Joy told Carmella as she reached into the cabinet and pulled out the fancy china that Carmella only used for family events.

"Why do you always use your best china for us, but use the regular plates for other guests?" Raven asked.

Carmella smiled. She hadn't known that her family noticed her preferences until Joy pulled the right plates out of the cabinet and then Raven commented about it. "You all are the most important people in my life; I wouldn't dare offer anything but the best to my family." She grabbed hold of Raven's arm, looked her in the eyes and said, "And don't you dare accept anything but the best from the man you choose to marry. You let him know that you're treated like royalty at home and the only way he can get your heart is if he can do better than what your father and I already do."

"You didn't tell me to say any of that to the men I dated," Joy complained.

"Girl, you didn't date all that much and you know it. But by the time you met Lance, I knew he was the one and I knew he would treat you like a queen. So, I didn't need to give you anything to say. I just kept praying that you would wake up and see what was right in front of you." And besides, Carmella had other reasons for saying what she had to Raven. The girl was beautiful, talented and smart, but she had an insecurity about her that caused Carmella to worry that she might let any old riffraff in her life. She didn't want Raven mentally or physically abused by any man, so she kept praying for her daughter.

Smiling as she gazed at the band on her finger, Joy said, "You were right about Lance. That man is so good for me and to me. I'm just glad that I finally gave him a chance."

"Me too," Raven said joyfully, "Your wedding was one of the best I've ever attended, and certainly the best that I ever served as maid of honor for... wait. Did I mention that?"

"Yes, you did," Joy said as she tried to hold in a giggle.

"Forget I said that. I'm throwing all my bridesmaid dressing away. I hereby declare that I will never be another bridesmaid." Raven held her hand up as if she was testifying before congress.

"Here, here," Joy seconded.

Carmella said, "I've already spoken to the good Lord on your behalf; so, believe me when I tell you, Raven, your time is coming." Carmella then picked up the platter holding the roast she had made; roast was Ramsey Jr.'s favorite. "Now, will you ladies help me set the table?"

***

"Man, am I glad to see you. That flight had me calling on the name of Jesus and confessing all my sins," Ramsey Jr. said as he got into Dontae's Range Rover.

"Boy, quit lying. That was only an hour flight, hardly enough time for you to confess *all* the stuff you've done... Don't forget, I know you."

"Shut up and get me away from this airport."

Dontae pulled away from the curb and began driving out of the airport lot. "Flight was that bad, huh?"

"I'm telling you, Dontae, if your Mama wasn't the praying woman that she is, I'd probably be gone on to glory right now."

"Her prayers don't always work; you do know that, don't you." Dontae spoke like a man who'd had first-hand experience in the prayers-not-getting-answered department.

"Real talk... your moms has helped me get through some things these last few years. All of her prayers seem to be working for me." Ramsey Jr. spread out his arms and looked around at the tree lined scenery as Dontae continued driving. "I'm back in North Carolina, aren't I?"

"Where the pollen is high and the women want more than a brother can give."

"I feel a sneeze coming on now. But that's all right. It's only unbearable for about the first couple weeks of spring."

"At least flowers are blooming all over the place in Charlotte," Dontae commented.

"I can hardly wait to get there."

Dontae came to a red light. He stopped the car and turned to his step-brother. "I was thinking..." He hesitated, and then charged on in, "that since you'll be staying with me for a while, I want to introduce you to one of Jewel's sisters. We can double date or something."

Ramsey adamantly shook his head. "Not interested, bro. I just shook off a woman who I didn't know was bipolar until she came at me with a knife. I'm still trying to get my head together from that."

"Come on, Ramsey, I need your help."

With furrowed brows, Ramsey asked, "What are you talking about? Since when do you need help with Jewel? The two of you have been into each other from the moment you met."

Dontae wished he didn't have to talk about what happened between him and Jewel, but he was desperate to get her back and needed help from his brother to make it happen. "We broke up."

"What do you mean, you broke up? You just bought her an engagement ring two weeks ago."

"She gave it back. Got upset when I handed her the prenup."

"I told you it was a bad idea."

"Look, I love Jewel and all, but I'm not about to give her half my money if she decides to leave me for some other man twenty years from now."

"You are such a cynic," Ramsey said, laughing at Dontae's comment.

"No. I'm a realist. And Jewel needs to understand just how real things could get if she or I ever decide to divorce."

"Wow. You and Jewel haven't even gotten married yet, and you're already thinking about divorce."

"Hey, I'm just being a realistic."

"No," Ramsey said, "You're just being cynical and trying to make Jewel pay for something that happened before she met you."

Dontae knew that Ramsey spoke the truth. His father had caused him to be a bit jaded. But dealing with a woman like Tory had also caused Dontae to doubt the reality of happily-ever-after. Once things weren't going the way she wanted them to go, he wasn't hearing sweet nothings from her anymore... seemed like the love Tory had for him just got up and left. If Jewel ever flipped a switch and started acting like Tory, he'd be heartbroken, but he'd still have his money to keep him company, which was why Jewel signing that prenuptial agreement was so important to him.

"Not to bring it up like this, but you are going to be staying at my house rent free. So, I think that one good turn deserves another."

"I'll pay rent if it's that big of a deal. I'm only going to be crashing with you long enough to find my own place anyway," Ramsey reminded Dontae.

Feeling guilty for the unnecessary comment, Dontae back tracked. "I'm not trying to charge you rent. I shouldn't have said it like that. I'm just desperate, man. Jewel is the one for me, so I really need your help."

"Just drop the whole prenup idea and your problem is solved."

Dontae shook his head. The look on his face was set, as if he was thinking about Michael Jordan, Kobe Bryant and all the other brothers who gambled and lost without a prenup. Oh sure, Kobe's wife stayed, but if she had pulled the trigger on that multi-million dollar divorce, Kobe would have been out hocking shirts, shoes and sodas to keep up with his standard of living. "I can't do that. Call me a fool. Call me jaded or whatever. But I just don't believe that people should go into marriage with their heart hanging out of their chest, without stopping to think about what could and probably would end up going wrong down the line."

"If I don't know nothing else, I know about things going horribly wrong," Ramsey said as he leaned back in his seat.

Dontae and Ramsey were both sinfully handsome and successful young men. But they had both experienced trauma that had changed their view of love, faith and God's ability to handle the things that concerned them. As smart as they were, neither man knew how to get out of his own way.

Ramsey popped up. "Ronny's traveling back to Charlotte with us. He's going to help me get my stuff set up in your house and in a storage unit."

"I can help you with that," Dontae said.

"Not with that knee of yours, you can't. I'm not going to be the one responsible for getting Carmella's boy all banged up again."

"What I mean is, we can pay a service to handle that for you."

"Naw, that's okay. Ronny just lost another job and I'd like to be able to put some money in his hands. And I'd like to spend some time with him before I start my new job. I told dad that I'd figure out what Ronny's next move should be."

Pulling into his mother's driveway, Dontae turned off the car and then asked Ramsey, "Do you think Ronny will help me out?"

Ramsey laughed. "Two women are involved, right?"

Dontae smiled at that. Ronny was definitely a ladies' man. "I forgot who we were talking about." Dontae nodded toward the front door. "You go on in, the family's waiting on you. I'm going to give Jewel's sister a call and tell her it's a go."

Ramsey put his hand on Dontae's shoulder. He had a sincere look on his face as he said, "I know we've only been brothers for the last eight years, but I just want you to know that I'm glad that we are family."

"Yeah, me too," Dontae said as he pulled his cell phone out and made a call to the woman he hoped would be his future sister-in-law.

The first person Dontae saw as he stepped into the house was Lance, his sister's husband. They shook hands and then Lance told him, "Man, am I glad you and Ramsey are here. I'm hungrier than a hostage and Carmella said we couldn't eat until you two rock heads got here."

"Stop." Dontae put up a hand. "I don't think I can handle all the love you're throwing my way."

"Don't get it twisted," Lance told him, "Family is good, but when you're hungry and your mother-in-law cooks like an Iron Chef, food is better."

The two men laughed as they joined the rest of the family. Carmella was busily uncovering the food as Dontae walked into the dining room. She turned and caught a glimpse of her son and then got the biggest grin on her face. "Come on in here, boy. I been waiting all day to give you a hug."

Even though his heart was heavy because of the situation with Jewel, Dontae yet and still smiled back at his mother. He could only remember one time in his life when his mother hadn't been there for him. With the horror stories he'd heard from other men about the things their mothers had done to them, Dontae wasn't about to dwell on one incident. "Hey Moms, I'm happy to see you, too," he said as they hugged. As he peeked over her shoulder, he added, "but I'm even happier to see that mac and cheese on the table."

"See Mom, I told you that I should be your favorite. This boy would take food over you," Joy said as she walked over and hugged her brother.

"Stop all that foolish talk, Joy Lynn. I have been blessed with seven children, two by birth and five by marriage and I love you all with a mother's heart," Carmella declared for everyone's hearing.

After that the family sat down to dinner. They talked, laughed and then played Trivia and Sequence. The ones who weren't playing either game got comfortable on the sofa and watched a movie. If anyone had looked into the Marshall household ten years ago, they never would have believed that all that sadness and dysfunction would one day turn into great joy.

As Ronny, Ramsey and Dontae stood, preparing to take that two hour drive from Raleigh to Charlotte, Carmella remembered something that she needed to tell Dontae. Ramsey and Ronny walked out to the car and Carmella grabbed hold of Dontae's arm and pulled him to the side. "Guess who I saw yesterday?"

Dontae gave her a blank stare. "I wouldn't know where to begin."

"Okay, okay... Coach Linden moved back to town. The school has hired him back and they are throwing an awards banquet for him." The excitement shone through with every word Carmella spoke.

Dontae didn't say anything.

Bringing her excitement down a notch or two, Carmella said, "I thought you'd want to know. I asked him to send the invitations to the banquet to my house because I thought you would want to attend."

A storm was brewing in Dontae's eyes as he said, "I don't want to attend. And I don't want you to go either." He turned and walked out of the house without further explanation.

2

"Oh no, that's not about to happen. Don't even worry about it. One hundred percent, I got your back." Dontae was on the phone with one of his clients while Ramsey and Ronny got themselves situated in the house.

"Thanks, Mr. Marshall. My dad was a little worried about me taking the meeting by myself, and he'll be out of town on business that weekend, so he can't attend."

"Your dad was right to worry. But I got this. I will contact Coach Jones and let him know that I will be making your hotel arrangements and setting the agenda for this meeting. Then if all goes well, you just might be the first round draft pick this year."

"That would be so awesome. I can't thank you enough, Mr. Marshall."

"Do me a favor. Stop calling me Mr. Marshall. In a year's time you'll be making so much money, people will be calling you mister. But the thing about it is, if you never forget what it felt like when you had to call others mister, you'll do just fine."

"I get it, I get it," his client said, then finished with, "Stay humble."

"Yeah, but don't be so humble that you end up missing the money being thrown your way." Dontae knew first hand that a career could end within minutes of getting started. But if a player was smart and grabbed hold of opportunities, he could make enough money to feed his family for a lifetime.

"I'll remember that, Mr.—I mean, Dontae."

"And no matter what happens next weekend, I'm getting you on a plane the minute the meeting is over. Under no circumstances do you agree to hang out with anyone for golf or anything else. You got me?" Dontae was firm on that. Owners and coaches tried to get over on kids fresh off the school bus. But Dontae made sure that his clients were protected from all the nonsense.

"Okay. My dad said the same thing."

"Your dad is a smart man." That made Dontae think about his own father. Nelson Marshall would be getting out of prison in about ten days. Dontae could only hope that he had finally wised up.

After hanging up with his client, Dontae walked into the family room where his brothers were resting. He made one more call; this one to his assistant. When Brielle answered the phone, he instructed her to contact his client's coach and inform him that he was the agent of record and would be attending the meeting. He then told her to make separate reservations for him and his client at the Ritz Carlton in Charleston, South Carolina for the following weekend.

"I love Charleston," Ronny said.

"And I love you for agreeing to help me out with my little problem. Unlike some other folk who shall remain nameless." Dontae pointedly stared at Ramsey as he switched from business mode to personal.

"Hey, we're family; why wouldn't I help you," Ronny said while leaning back in his seat on the family room sofa in Dontae's condo.

"Oh, yeah right," Ramsey Jr. scoffed, "And if Jewel's sister had been ugly, I bet you would have forgot all about this we-are-family moment you're having."

Ronny looked as if Ramsey had misjudged and falsely accused him. He put his hands on his chest. "I'm trying to take one for the team. At least I'm willing to help Dontae with his sad and pathetic love life."

"Hey, there's nothing sad or pathetic about my love life," Dontae objected. "At least I have a woman. I'm the one setting you up with a woman."

Ronny stood up, popped his collar as he strutted around the room. "Don't need help with the ladies. I'm doing you a favor."

Ronny was mostly correct. Being young and handsome, the three men needed little help where the ladies were concerned. However, what Ronny lacked was focus. He had an entrepreneurial mindset, but floated around from one idea to the next, never sticking with anything long enough to see it through to the other side of success. Dontae hoped that being around him and Ramsey this week would help his step-brother focus and figure out what he wanted to do with his life.

"Okay, you're right. You are doing me a favor and I thank you," Dontae conceded so they could get on with it. "Now, since you're such a ladies' man, help me pick out a restaurant where I can arrange for us to run into Jewel and Dawn."

"Hold on, Playa," Ronny took center stage again. "Didn't you tell us that Jewel threw those prenup papers in your face while y'all was at a restaurant? And you want to just simply bump into her at another one? What you want her to do at this restaurant, throw her drink in your face?"

"What's the man supposed to do, Ronny? He's got to run into her somewhere, because she's not taking his calls right now. And Jewel is a Christian woman, he won't find her hanging out at some rump shaking night club," Ramsey said.

"Just shaking my head." Ronny walked over to Dontae's laptop and turned it on. He then turned back to Dontae with confusion written on his face. "How do you use this thing?"

Dontae got up, walked over to the table. "You've never used a Mac before?"

"I'm a starving entrepreneur, where would I get the money to buy anything that comes out of the Apple store?" He pulled his cell phone out of his pocket and said, "I'm still using my flip phone."

Dontae and Ramsey had no problem laughing in Ronny's face.

"Laugh if you want to, but when Sprint told me I had a relic of a phone and tried to get me to upgrade, I told them I would wait until Beyoncé decided to upgrade me herself."

"You gon' be waiting a long time, bro. I think Beyoncé is happy where she's at. And anyway, you don't want none of that baby's daddy drama," Dontae said, laughing, but as he turned in Ramsey's direction to get a co-signer on his joke, Dontae caught a glimpse of sadness in Ramsey's eyes that took the fun out of the moment. Dontae was about to ask Ramsey if he was alright, but then Ronny got his attention.

"A notification of an email from Mama Carmella just popped up."

"Just ignore it, click on Safari and go on to the website you want me to see," Dontae told him.

Ronny shook his head. "Can't just ignore Mama Carmella's emails. She delivers some real nuggets." Ronny opened his flip phone. "If you're not going to check your email, I'm going to check mine so I can read her Praise Alert for the day."

Dontae rolled his eyes heavenward. His mother emailed her so-called Praise Alerts out to the family at least once a week. His step-father's children all seemed to enjoy receiving the Praise Alerts; they even sent comments back. Dontae wished they would stop hitting reply to all because he wasn't really interested.

All these Praise Alerts were his sister, Joy's fault. About five years ago, his mother had given Joy a journal to write down her thoughts and to give God praise for things He had done in her life. At the time, Joy wasn't really feeling it. However, within a few months his sister had given her life to the Lord and gotten over some serious issues in her life. Ever since that happened, his mother decided that the entire family needed to be in on this praise thing. Hence the Praise Alerts.

"Get up, boy. Let me open my email so you don't have to strain your eyes trying to read it on that 1999 flip phone."

Ronny got up and then hovered over Dontae's shoulder while he opened his email account. Ramsey came and stood behind Dontae also. They each read the Praise Alert at the same time. Her Praise Alerts always began with a scripture out of Psalm 150:

Praise ye the Lord. Praise God in his sanctuary: praise Him in the firmament of his power. Praise Him for His mighty acts; praise Him according to His excellent greatness... Let every thing that hath breath praise the Lord. Praise ye the Lord.

After the scripture the praise alert went on to tell of God's goodness in someone else's life. This one said, '*For the past three years I have gone through so much. I went from being blessed and having everything, well at least materialistically (cars, homes, a great job), to having nothing, not even hot water to bathe—not that I wanted to because I was so depressed. My wife left me and my house was due to be sold on March 4th (foreclosure) and today I was approved for SSDI and they are working with me and Legal Aid to see how they can help to save my home. Imagine, the SS Administration trying to help. I don't know why God brought me so low, but I pray that it is for His glory. Oh and I also thank Him for giving me a fighting spirit that will not allow any demonic influences or energies to win. My wife said that my fighting spirit was what won her heart back... Praise the Lord!*

"Mama Carmella is something else," Ramsey Jr. said as he finished reading the Praise Alert.

"Tell me about it," Ronny added. "There have been days when I've been down on myself about my business and then she'd send one of her Praise Alerts and it just picked me right up."

Dontae wasn't as enthusiastic. He stood up, pointed to his seat and asked Ronny, "Can you show me the website you wanted me to check out now?"

"Oh, sure thing." Ronny sat back down and typed an address in the browser, hit enter and then pointed at the screen as the information materialized.

"The Sanctuary at Kiawah Island?" Dontae had a puzzled look on his face.

"Why you got your face all scrunched up like that? It's a five-star resort. What better place to win your lady back?"

"I'm not saying the place isn't nice. But it's all the way in Charleston, South Carolina. I just don't see why we have to leave Charlotte when both Jewel and I already live here."

"Just shaking my head," Ronny said again.

"What? What did I say?" Dontae turned to Ramsey for help.

Ronny said, "You're going to Charleston next weekend anyway. I just heard you book the Ritz for business. Why not schedule something with Jewel after your meeting."

"I'll tell you why," Dontae said. "There's going to be a ton of athletes in Charleston networking and cheesing for the camera that weekend. How can I concentrate on Jewel with all that going on?"

"That's why I'm suggesting The Sanctuary. Your meeting is at the Ritz. Once we check out of there... it's all about personal," Ronny said.

"I don't know, D, I'm kind of with Ronny on this one." Ramsey scrolled down, looking at the features the resort offered. "To me, if you just run into her at a restaurant in Charlotte, that doesn't seem like you put a lot of effort into it. But run into her at a swank place that this... and then she discovers that you set the whole thing up, now that sounds like a man who wants his woman back."

"How would I even get Jewel to agree to meet me at this resort?"

"You won't," Ronny said, then added, "Book the rooms for this weekend, then have Dawn tell her that she has a free weekend at a five-star resort. Jewel will bite because she's ticked with you and probably needs a little getaway right now."

Dontae took a moment to think it over, then said, "Actually, this isn't a bad idea." He turned to Ramsey and added, "So glad you invited Ronny out here this week. Looks like he's going to be helping both of us."

"He wasn't doing anything else. Might as well help us out," Ramsey said.

"Glad that my between-jobs situation could be of service to my brothers. But since we all know that I don't have any money... I might be charging for my services this week."

***

Jewel's eyes were just about popping out of her head as she and Dawn pulled up to The Sanctuary resort at Kiawah Island. The valet opened the car doors for them, then about two or three other employees said, "Welcome to The Sanctuary," as they made their way up the walkway. The front doors were pulled open by staff members as they approached. As they entered the large main entrance, Jewel couldn't help but be awed by her beautiful surroundings. Looked like a place where royalty vacationed.

As they walked through the doors, three more staff members welcomed them to The Sanctuary and then directed them to the registration desk. "Girl, this place is top notch. How on earth did you get a free stay at a resort like this?"

"Don't look a gift horse in the mouth. Let's just enjoy the weekend. Didn't you tell me that you needed to get away?"

"I had no idea that you would bring me to a place like this. All I can say is, you must really love me and I might need to break up with the love of my life about once a year if I get perks like this for my troubles."

Dawn took the room key from the desk clerk and as she and Jewel headed to their room she asked, "So you think this weekend will make up for your broken engagement?"

Jewel stopped, put her hand over her heart and shook her head. "Forget what I just said. I don't ever want to go through this kind of pain again in life."

"I'm sorry that I asked you that, Jewel. Please forgive me." Dawn put her arms around her sister and lovingly pulled her into an embrace. "I shouldn't have said that.

Please just forget what I said and let's try to enjoy ourselves this weekend."

Jewel drew strength from the hug. She took a deep breath and then stepped back. "I'm good. I don't want to spoil our fun this weekend by dwelling on my problems with Dontae."

"That's the spirit," Dawn said as she they found their room and she opened the door.

Taking in the beauty of the suite, and walking from the living room, to the kitchen and then the bedroom, Jewel said, "The only way I can see you getting this room for free is if they think they are going to get about thirty grand off of you by suckering you into one of those timeshares."

"Girl please, I don't make enough money to even qualify for a timeshare."

Still walking around, taking in every facet of the suite, Jewel said, "Well you sure must be living right or something. God is in the blessing business and I guess he just decided to bless us this weekend."

"In more ways than one, my dear sister... in more ways than one," Dawn said without even cracking a smile.

3

"Man, you wasn't lying. This is hot," Dontae said as they stepped inside the resort.

As they walked to the registration desk, several staff members said, "Welcome to The Sanctuary.

"I told you that this spot was legit. Now come on. Let's hurry up and get the key to our rooms so we can get ready for our golf game."

Dontae stood flat footed and looked around the lobby area. "Why would you sign us up for golf? Jewel doesn't play and won't be anywhere near the greens."

"Will you stop thinking about your love life for a minute? We can do a little networking on the golf course and then we can do lunch on the beach at the Loggerhead Grill. They are supposed to have really good burgers and Dawn said that she'll have Jewel on the beach as we stroll towards the grill."

"All right, all right. That sounds like a plan." Dontae was anxious to see Jewel and make things right. But he didn't want to blow his chances. She'd been refusing to see or talk to him for two weeks now.

They went to their rooms to get changed. Dontae showered, threw on a pair of tan shorts and a white polo shirt. He pulled out his iPad to check his emails, never know when another endorsement deal might come through for one of his clients. Dontae didn't like to sleep on those types of things. His clients were pro-ballers, they made good money in the NBA and NFL; however, most of them longed for the big money that endorsements could bring, so he was always on the lookout.

While scrolling through his emails, Dontae noticed that someone from his old high school had emailed him concerning Coach Linden's awards banquet. Dontae deleted the email without opening it.

He then went through the rest of the emails, quickly answering questions and jotting down notes. As he was finishing up, he received another Praise Alert from his mother. Dontae was about to close down his computer without even opening it, but then he remembered how excited Ramsey Jr. and Ronny were to receive the Praise Alerts and he felt a little guilty.

He opened the Praise Alert and read from Psalm 150 again:

... Let every thing that hath breath praise the Lord. Praise ye the Lord.

The Praise Alert read, '*I found an article in a reader's digest when I was 13; it was a guaranteed formula for getting the results you want from prayer. So I said this prayer believing for a miracle, and it worked, and I heard the voice of Jesus in a dream, assuring me that everything would be okay. This would be the first of many miracles over a span of nearly two decades. You see, ever since that very first miracle, I never had peace, contentment or fulfillment in my life. In fact I was unhappy and depressed for most of that time because God was only in my life as a provider of material needs, like a year-round Santa. But I praise Him today, because He stayed faithful giving me miracle after miracle after miracle, because he never changes or writes us off, even when we deserve it. He is the same yesterday, today and forever and his word is infallible, claim it in faith and it never fails you. Mark 11:24 reminds us that Jesus never told a lie. Whatever you ask for in faith, you will receive. But remember that things can never take the place of God in your life. If you want the peace that surpasses all understanding, seek Jesus, not just as savior, but also as Lord.*'

Where does she find this stuff? Dontae wondered. But then he just put it out of his head. He'd read the Praise Alert. Now if one of his step-brothers mentioned his mother's Praise Alert at least he'd be able to say he read it also... read, but that's about it. Nothing in the email spoke to him or caused him to bless the Lord. Dontae had grown up in church, but sometimes he felt numb to it all.

He turned off his iPad, put it back in his suitcase and then grabbed his golf clubs. He was almost out the door when his cell phone rang. It was his mother. He opened the door to his hotel room as he answered the phone. "Hey Mama, what's up?"

"And how are you on this most wondrous day?" Carmella asked her son.

"I'm doing all right. Getting ready to golf with Ronny."

"That's good. Well, I don't want to hold you up. I was just calling to tell you that your sister said that your father will definitely be released on Tuesday."

"I didn't think he'd be out until Thursday. Thanks for letting me know. I'll try my best to get back there so I can see him next week."

"Good. Your father will need you and your sister even more than you know. And I'm proud that both of you have a mind to be there for him."

"Careful Mom, you actually sound like you care."

"Of course I care about your father. I was married to the man for over twenty years."

And then he left you for a woman who was barely in her twenties at the time, Dontae thought but wouldn't dare say to his mother. So he chose to say instead, "I just got your Praise Alert."

"What'd you think of that one?"

"Honestly Mom, I really don't know what to think. I don't even know why you send those alerts."

"You really don't know?"

"I really don't, but I wish you would enlighten me. And where do you get all those stories from?"

Carmella hesitated for a moment, then said, "Different people send me praise reports or I find them on the internet. But I sent them because I want all of you to know God."

Continuing down the hall towards the lobby, Dontae said, "Oh, well then you don't need to send those alerts to me, because I already know God."

"No," Carmella said with force, "you know about *my* God. I want you to come to know *your* God."

That sounded strange to Dontae. After attending church all of his life, how could his mother say that he didn't know God? He almost asked her for clarification, but then he ran into Ronny and decided to table the conversation for another time. "I'll call you back later, Mom. Ronny is ready to take his whoopin' on the golf course."

"Okay Son, I love you and tell Ronny I love him also."

"I'm not getting ready to tell a grown man that. But I will give him the phone so you can tell him yourself." Dontae passed his cell to Ronny.

Ronny gripped the phone to his ear, smiled and then said, "I love you, too, Mama Carmella."

Dontae took the phone back. "Love you, Mom. I'll see you next week." He hung up his cell and then he and Ronny headed to the golf course. Dontae proceeded to show everyone just how off focus his game was.

By the time they reached the fifth hole, Ronny was frustrated enough to ask, "What's wrong with you? You're not even trying to make us look good out here."

"I'm here aren't I?" He pointed at Micah and Drake, the two men they were playing against. "Go on back over there and continue telling them about your next get-rich-quick scheme."

"Oh it's like that, huh?"

"Yeah, it's like that," Dontae said as he lifted his club and prepared to swing and missed.

"Maybe you'd hit a few balls if you didn't have such a nasty disposition." Dontae scowled at him. Ronny shrugged his shoulders. "I'm just saying." He walked over to the other team and said, "Looks like it's y'all's turn again, since my partner can't seem to hit wind, let alone a little old golf ball."

That was it, Dontae had taken all he could from his younger brother. He threw down his gold club, swung around and charged at Ronny like he was still playing football. "I bet I could hit *you* with no problem at all."

Ronny's eyes widened. He held up a hand as Dontae approached. "What's with all this aggression? I'm not about to fight you. I'll fight the world with you, but I wasn't raised like this. I'm not about to come to blows with my own brother."

Dontae backed up, took a deep breath as he unclenched his fists. Dontae and Ronny hadn't been raised in the same household, but Ronny was right. For almost a decade now, they had been brothers, and he was grateful for the new brothers and sisters that he now had. "I'm sorry about that, bro. I just don't know why I get so angry at times."

Micah and Drake both glanced at their watches and then Micah said, "Hey, we've had a lot of fun with the game, but we probably need to get back. Got a meeting scheduled in an hour."

"It's cool," Ronny said. The two men began walking away from them as fast as they could, as Ronny threw in, "Go ahead and chock this one up as a win for your team, Micah."

"Sorry about that, Ronny. I know you were trying to pitch to the investment banker. But my heart just wasn't in the game."

"Oh well. Easy come, easy go." Ronny slapped a hand on Dontae's shoulder and said, "Come on, let's go grab some lunch."

***

Lounging on the beach in her purple and tan bikini, Jewel felt as if she'd been swept away to a place of peace where the problems she had back in Charlotte didn't even matter. "Thanks for inviting me to this wonderful place. I feel so at peace here," Jewel said as she turned to her sister, who lay beside her.

"You're the only person I wanted to come here with."

Jewel laughed. "You don't have me fooled for a minute, Dawn. You are lying on the lounge chair right now, dreaming about Taye Diggs rounding that corner." She pointed towards the entrance over by the Loggerhead Grill. "And then walking by us, stopping as he catches a glimpse of you, and then dropping down on one knee and asking you to marry him."

Dawn waved the thought away. "Get real, Jewel. In case you forgot, Taye Diggs likes white women. He's been married to one for over ten years, so I don't have any illusions about him or anyone else getting all excited about seeing me."

Jewel sat up. She grabbed her sister's hand and pulled her up with her. "What are you talking about, Dawn? Don't you know how beautiful you are?"

Dawn averted her eyes.

"I'm serious. You always put yourself down about one thing or another. But you have got it going on and I think it's about time you accepted that fact."

"I know that I'm smart. But I'm just not as pretty as you and Maxine."

Maxine was their oldest sister and she was something to see. Long legs, slender body and a face that Halle Berry would kill for. But that didn't mean that Jewel and Dawn were throw-backs. "Okay, our sister is a model and we're not, but we are still desirable women. I know my worth, what about you, Dawn Henderson?"

"You don't know what it's like being a sister to you and Maxine," Dawn complained.

"And you don't know what it's like being a sister to a magna cum laude graduate both in high school and college. Then that same sister becomes this awesome engineer who helped design the car that I drive every day."

"Okay, okay. You win. Yes, I know my worth. I am fabulous. So, don't try to throw Taye Diggs off on me... now if Idris Elba came around that corner looking for a woman to love, I just might have to rescue that brother."

"Not if I see him first," Jewel said, giggling. She liked the sound of her laughter. She hadn't heard that sound in the past two weeks.

"Oh please," Dawn said, "You already have a man wanting to marry you, so you don't need to steal my Idris Elba dreams away from me."

Thinking of Dontae sucked all the joy out of Jewel's day. She stretched back out on the lounge chair and stared at the pool that was not more than a foot or two away from where she lay. She then turned her attention to heaven above, praying for answers that never seemed to come. She didn't understand the man she had fallen in love with, not one single bit. But she prayed that the love she had for Dontae Marshall would not torment her for the rest of her days.

"I'm sorry, Jewel. I didn't mean to make you sad all over again. I was just joking with you."

Jewel wished that she was at church so she could go down to the altar and lay herself prostrate before God and allow Him to heal her wounded heart.

Dawn cleared her throat. Tapped Jewel's arm and said, "Look, we're right here at the Loggerhead Grill. Why don't we grab some lunch and then go back to our room and get dressed so we can do some shopping this afternoon?"

Tempted to just lay there and wallow in self-pity for at least another hour, Jewel almost turned down her sister's game plan, but then she gave herself a silent pep talk and then slapped her hands together as she sat back up. "That sounds like a plan."

Just as two men rounded the corner, entering the pool area, Jewel bent down to pick up the straw hat she'd laid on the ground. She put the hat back on her head and then slid her feet in her shoes, bending to adjust the strap. As she rose back up, she startled as out of the corner of her eye she spotted someone close behind her—too close. She swung around and came face to face with Dontae.

Forgetting her close proximity to the pool, she moved back to allow more space between them, but losing her footing at the pool's edge, her arms began flailing. Dontae reached out and tried to grab hold of Jewel's arm, but she was, by then, too far out of his reach, so he leaned forward a bit to catch her. Jewel grabbed hold of Dontae about a second before she fell backward into the pool, taking Dontae with her.

"Dontae, what are you doing here?" Jewel asked as they wiped water from their eyes and then looked each other in the face.

"Looks like I'm about to go for a swim with you," Dontae said good naturedly.

But Jewel wasn't having it. She smelled a rat, and had a feeling that Dawn would be ordering a bowl full of cheese for lunch today.

4

Jewel toweled off and then walked a few feet away from the pool to sit down at one of the outdoor tables at the Loggerhead Grill.

Dontae pulled his shirt over his head, wrung it out a few times and then flung it over his shoulder as he joined Jewel and Dawn at the table. As Ronny sat down, Dontae said, "You remember Ronny, don't you, Jewel?"

Jewel gave Ronny a tight lipped smile. "Of course I remember Ronny. How is your travel business going?"

Ronny shook his head. "People just aren't traveling as much these days, what with the economic meltdown this country has gone through."

"Tell me about it," Dawn agreed. "This is the first time I've gotten out of Charlotte in a year."

Ronny held out a hand to Dawn. "I'm Ronny, Dontae's younger brother."

Shaking his hand, Dawn said, "I'm Jewel's younger sister... oh, my name is Dawn."

"Dawn." Ronny let the name roll off his tongue and he released her hand. "Such a beautiful name for an equally beautiful woman."

Before Dawn had time to blush, the waiter arrived at their table with their menus. They each studied the menus for a moment and then Jewel ordered the fish tacos. Her plan was to eat them and then blow all of her fish taco breath in Dontae's direction.

Dontae ordered the pulled pork; Ronny ordered a burger, while Dawn ordered the Cobb salad. As they handed the menus back to the waiter, Jewel pointedly asked, "So, what brings you two here this weekend?"

"Oh, just doing a little networking. We just left the golf course, talking with a few potential clients," Dontae answered.

"Is that right?" Jewel said while glancing at her sister.

Dawn fidgeted nervously. "Isn't this just wonderful that we all ended up here together?"

"Yes, isn't it just wonderful." Jewel decided to take care of her sister later. For now, she was just going to get through the lunch with Dontae and then go on about her business. But it really bothered her that he would spend so much money on this so-called "free" weekend resort getaway, while at the same time, he was worried that she was going to divorce him and try to take all of his money. He confused her.

They ate their meals with Ronny doing most of the talking. If she had learned nothing else about Dontae's step-brother, she knew that he was a talker. Jewel thought he'd make a great car salesman, could probably even do well enough to buy his own dealership. But who was she to tell him how to run his life. She couldn't even figure out what to do with her own life.

As they were finishing up their meal, the waiter came back to the table and asked, "Does anyone want dessert?"

Jewel wiped her mouth with her napkin. "No, thank you. Can you please bring the bill?"

"Not a problem," he said, then asked, "Will this be on one bill?"

Dontae said, "Yes."

Jewel quickly lifted a hand and said, "No." She then pointed to Dawn and told the waiter, "Make it two. I'll pay for her, and then you can give them," she pointed toward Dontae and Ronny, "their own bill."

When the waiter walked away, Dontae leaned toward Jewel, put his hand on her thigh. "Why won't you let me pay for your lunch?"

She removed his hand. "Don't you think you've paid for enough?"

Back in their room, Jewel gave Dawn an earful. "How could you lie to me like this, Dawn?"

"I didn't lie to you," Dawn protested.

"You most certainly did. I asked you numerous times how you were able to swing not just a hotel room, but a suite in this wildly expensive resort. You never once said that Dontae paid for our room." Dawn opened her mouth, Jewel pointed at her. "And don't you dare lie to me again. I know that you and Dontae planned this trip." Jewel wore out the carpet walking from one side of the room to the next. "He thinks he's got me cornered, but I'll show him."

Dawn flopped down on the bed. "Jewel, be reasonable. Dontae isn't trying to corner you. He just wants you to talk to him. The man really loves you."

"The man thinks I'm a gold digger," Jewel threw back at her sister. "I'm not putting up with being treated like that. My father never put a price tag on his love for Mama... and no man that truly loves me would do something as horrible as that either."

Jewel, I understand why you're upset. And you are right. Daddy has always told us not to sell ourselves short with the men we date. But I don't think Dontae meant anything by what he did. People in his circle have prenups drawn up all the time."

"Well then, maybe he needs to change his circle of friends." Jewel shook her head and lifted her hands. "I'm getting in the shower." She went into the bathroom and jumped in the shower. Walking out of the bathroom, Jewel threw on a sundress and was about to sit down so she and her sister could continue their conversation.

But Dawn had other plans. She grabbed her purse. "Let's just go shopping and enjoy the rest of our day.

Sighing heavily, Jewel put her purse on her shoulder and left the room with her sister. Jewel was trying her best to forgive her sister for what she considered a betrayal of sisterhood. She had told Dawn how Dontae had boldly handed her a prenuptial agreement, moments after she had joyfully agreed to marry him. He hadn't even let her enjoy the moment before shoving a document in her face, which let her know that he cared more about his money than he cared about her.

Why couldn't her family just stay out of her business and let her live her own life? But her parents thought that Dontae was a great catch. Both of her sisters gushed over how wonderful she and Dontae look together... the perfect couple they all claimed. But Jewel had her doubts because if they were so perfect for each other, why would Dontae have his mind fixated on some divorce that should never happen anyway?

"Please don't be mad at me," Dawn said a second before they rounded the corner and entered the lobby.

Jewel was about to tell her sister that she would eventually get over her anger, after some prayer and fasting, but then she saw Dontae and Ronny standing in the lobby looking at her as if she had kept them waiting for some important meeting or something.

"Why are they waiting on us?" Jewel asked Dawn.

"That's why I asked you not to be mad at me," Dawn whispered, "Dontae called while you were in the shower. I happened to mention that we were getting ready to go shopping." When Jewel gave her the evil eye, Dawn said, "I'm sorry. I promise I won't tell him anything else."

Jewel wagged a finger at her sister, the traitor. "You better not."

"Ladies, just consider me your driver for the day," Dontae said as he bowed gallantly in front of them.

"Dawn drove, so we don't need your help." Jewel walked past Dontae and stepped outside.

Dontae rushed behind her. "Come on, Jewel, look," he pointed towards his Range Rover. "My SUV is already here and waiting on you. Dawn's car is still in the parking garage. And don't forget, if you purchase a bunch of things while you're out today, Dawn's little BMW won't have enough room to hold all your things."

"My car is pretty small compared to Dontae's SUV," Dawn said.

Jewel gave her the evil eye again.

"Just saying." Dawn hunched her shoulders.

"I'll trade you," Ronny offered.

"What do you drive?" Dawn asked.

"Ever since my car broke down, I've been driving these." Ronny lifted his feet to show what he was working with.

"And you think I would trade the Beemer I worked hard to get so that I could walk myself back and forth to work, church and the grocery store?" Dawn didn't even wait on an answer from Ronny, she strutted over to Jewel and said, "Do you want me to have my car brought out or are we going to ride with Dontae and the foot man?"

Throwing up her hands as if giving up, Jewel opened the passenger door and got in Dontae's car. "Let's just go."

Dontae climbed in the driver seat; while he put on his seat belt, Ronny and Dawn got in the back seat. "Which mall am I driving you lovely ladies to?"

"We're going to the outlet mall," Dawn answered.

Dontae turned to Jewel and tried to win some points by saying, "My baby don't have to shop the outlet malls looking for discounts. We can go straight to the regular mall, because I'm going to buy you whatever you want."

Jewel wasn't having it. The man shoved a prenup in her face and now he was acting like he wanted to buy her the world... if he did, she would take a shuttle to Mars. "I don't need your money. I'm just fine with shopping at the outlets and with spending my own money, thank you very much."

***

Dontae was tempted to call his Mama and ask her to pray for him because he was striking out right and left with Jewel. He had taken her to the outlet as she suggested, walked two steps behind her as she and Dawn explored each and every store they wanted to go into. He hadn't complained not even once about the three hours they spent going from store to store. But once they finished shopping and were back at the hotel, Dontae was starving so he invited Jewel and Dawn to have dinner with him and Ronny.

Dawn was getting ready to accept until Jewel said, "I wouldn't want to take up any more of your time or cause you to spend any of your precious money on someone like me."

Dontae put his hand on Jewel's arm and said, "I'm not worried about my money. I just want to take you to dinner."

All business like, she responded, "You're very kind to offer, but I'm going to do dinner with my sister tonight." Jewel grabbed Dawn's arm and began pulling her away. She waved at Dontae. "Thanks for taking us to the mall."

"Why does she keep harping on money?" Dontae asked, frustrated as he watched her walk away from him.

"Because you gave her that prenup, stupid," Ronny said as he put a hand on Dontae's shoulder. "You have really made Jewel mad. I'd say you've got a lot of begging to do."

Dontae removed Ronny's hand from his shoulder. "Get off me, man. I've been trying to make up with her. Didn't you see how she was today? She won't even talk to me."

"Why don't you just let her burn that prenup and then take her in your arms and show her how much you love her?"

"That all sounds wonderful when you're using your feet for transportation, but when you've got some real money to lose, not having a prenup doesn't make much sense." Dontae's dad had deserved what he'd gotten in the divorce settlement with his mother, because Nelson Marshall had cheated on Carmella. But even though Nelson Marshall was a cheater, a part of Dontae bled for his father, because he had to give up so much of his income in the divorce that the financial loss eventually became his undoing.

"If you love her, stop thinking about divorce and concentrate on how you can make a marriage with her work for a lifetime."

Dontae turned to his brother. The doubt in his eyes was evident as he said, "In this day and age, who can really last a lifetime in anything?"

5

"Mom, come on, I need your help," Joy whined as she sat in the kitchen with her mother.

Carmella's praise music was playing while she stirred the green beans she was cooking to go along with tonight's dinner. "I can't do it, Joy. Dontae told me flat out not to attend that awards banquet."

"Just because Dontae is ungrateful, doesn't mean that we can't go and celebrate a man who did so much for my brother and your son."

Carmella sat down next to Joy. "I agree with you, Joy. I think that Dontae not attending that banquet is rude beyond belief, but what can I do?"

"You and I can go in place of Dontae. Coach Linden will be grateful to see us, since he did send you an invitation as well as Dontae."

"I just don't know why it's such a big deal to you," Carmella said, eyeing her daughter.

"It's not a big deal to me. But Lance's law firm is in consideration for the school board contract. He wants to represent them in the worst way, and thinks that his showing up at this awards banquet might just give him the networking time needed to close the deal."

"So my son-in-law asked you to hit me up for the tickets?"

"Yes," Joy admitted. Then added, "But I need you to come with us, because I'm going to be bored out of my mind while Lance is floating around the room, collecting business cards and grinning at everybody."

Carmella tapped a finger on the counter, thinking how hard it was to please both her children at the same time. "Okay, I'll go. But I want to tell your brother myself, so don't go running your mouth."

"I couldn't if I wanted to. Dontae is out of town right now, and I'm not trying to bother him while he's on his mission."

"What mission?" Carmella had spoken to her son yesterday and he didn't act as if anything out of the ordinary was going on.

"Oh he didn't tell you?" Joy was practically giggling.

Carmella shook her head.

"I called Dontae's house so that I could tell him about his ungrateful self. I mean, who ever heard of not wanting to celebrate the very man who helped you get into the college of your choice, thereby allowing you to get drafted into the NFL. Essentially, Coach Linden is the reason Dontae is successful today."

Carmella held up a finger, stopping Joy for a moment. "I have to correct that, hon, because the God that this family serves is the reason me, you, Dontae and the rest of this family is successful."

"Okay, okay, you're right, Mom. So anyway, Ramsey told me that Dontae and Ronny were in Charleston trying to surprise Jewel and get her to take Dontae back."

One of Carmella's hands flew to her mouth while the other touched her heart. "Dontae really loves Jewel. And she is just right for him. I so hope that he is able to save that relationship."

"She's a heck of a lot better than that other one he wanted to marry. I'm just glad that Tory is out of the picture."

"You and me both."

***

Dontae and Ronny sat in the lobby trying to figure out where they would eat dinner. They had a few places to choose from, but Dontae wanted to make sure they picked the same restaurant where Jewel and Dawn would be dining that night. He'd tried to call Dawn to get that information from her, but Dawn wasn't answering her phone anymore.

"So what are we going to do, man? My stomach is growling."

"Go on to dinner without me. I can't get a hold of Dawn so I don't know where I should eat tonight. But I don't want to hold you up."

Ronny stood up, got ready to head out and then sat back down. "I can't just leave you like this. I'd never forgive myself if you went off and did something stupid." Slouching in his seat, Ronny said, "I'll just tell Mama Carmella that we spent the night fasting and praying; that ought to make her happy."

"I'm not praying. That stuff doesn't work," Dontae remarked.

Ronny gave Dontae a shame-shame kind of look. "Your mama would slap you if she heard what you just said. And anyway, who said anything about you praying. I'm the one over here praying for a nice thick steak, or a lobster... yeah, yeah, I'll just sit over here and pray for lobster."

Dontae rubbed his index finger around his chin while he took a moment to think things over. He turned back to Ronny and asked, "Do you think I should go up there and try to talk to her?"

Ronny laughed. "She has really got you all twisted up."

"Shut up, Ronny. If you're not going to help me, then why are you here?"

"I'm sorry about laughing. It's just that you're normally Mr. Got-it-all-together. I've never seen this side of you. Not even when you busted up your knee on the football field, and not even when you broke up with that girl, um…" Ronny started snapping his fingers trying to come up with the name.

Suddenly, Dontae stood up and said, "Tory…"

"Yeah, yeah, that was her name," Ronny was saying.

Dontae was looking at the woman in the flesh… well, not in the *flesh* flesh. Tory preferred to clothe herself in high end designers. And she wasn't slacking a bit that day. Had on an off white Sophie Theallet dress with a silk shoulder strap, coupled with the Gucci purse and shoes she was also rocking, he'd say that Tory had found herself another baller. Because she was definitely sporting at least three to four thou and Tory's credit was all jacked up, and since she'd dropped out of college, he knew that she couldn't afford those digs on her own. Matter-of-fact, his pockets were still hurting from all the money he'd laid out on her shopping sprees.

"What are you doing here?" he asked as she strutted over to him. She had a friend with her who was rocking Louis.

"Hanging out with friends for the weekend." She pointed to the woman standing next to her and said, "This is my girl, Diamond."

Dontae shook her hand. Ronny stood and shook hands with both women as Dontae introduced him.

Tory stood there for a moment, looking Dontae over as if he was a prized possession she had lost and then found behind the dresser or something. She then wrapped her arms around Dontae and squeezed him like she was in the fruits and vegetable aisle and was testing for freshness. "It's so good to see you." She then kissed his forehead, his cheek and was about to kiss his lips, but Dontae broke free and stepped away from her.

However, he hadn't broken free fast enough, because Ronny was tapping him on the shoulder and pointing toward the lobby entryway where Jewel and Dawn stood. Both women had their hands on their hips and fire in their eyes.

"Hey baby," Dontae said, as he stepped around Tory and rushed over to Jewel. He took her hand in his and walked her back over to where Tory and Ronny stood. "I don't think you met Tory before. But I told you about her. Remember... she was my—"

"I remember." Jewel pulled her hand away from Dontae and held it out for Tory. "I'm Jewel. How are you?"

"Honey, I'm always good, believe that." Tory shook Jewel's hand and then she and her friend began walking away. Before leaving the lobby, she turned back to Dontae and said, "Nice seeing you again. Don't be a stranger."

"Oh, I'm quite sure that he's going to be a stranger to you from here on out," Dawn said as Tory passed by her.

"Cat fight," Ronny said as he rushed over to Dawn and put his arm around her. "I'm going to keep you close to me, before you do something that will get your pretty little self arrested."

Stepping out of Ronny's embrace, Dawn said, "I'm not the one you need to be worried about." She walked over to Jewel and asked, "Are you all right?"

Jewel folded her arms across her chest as she glared at Dontae. "I'm fine."

"Look Jewel, I wasn't doing anything. Tory just showed up and before I knew anything she was hugging me."

"Looked like she was molesting you," Dawn said.

"Girl, you are quick on your feet. I think I'm falling in love," Ronny said while trying to lean closer to Dawn.

Dontae gave him the eye.

"Dontae is telling the truth," Ronny said. "He didn't do anything to provoke Tory to rub all up on him the way she did."

"Stop helping me, okay, Ronny?" Dontae said as he shook his head. He knew that he should have brought Ramsey Jr. instead of Ronny. His younger brother seemed to take pleasure in messing things up.

"Look Dontae, I think it might be best for Dawn and me to head back home."

"No Jewel, don't leave. I really wanted to spend some time with you this weekend so that we could talk." He looked around at a few of the people who were walking through the lobby. Dontae wanted to hold on to as much of his dignity as he had left. He wanted to play it cool, but the woman he loved was getting ready to pack up and walk out of his life again. He had to do something.

"What difference does it make, Dontae. We could talk all night long, but I don't think either one of us will change our minds."

Dontae wanted to pull out his eyeballs. Jewel was driving him up a wall. He grabbed hold of her arm and moved her toward the back of the room. He leaned in close to Jewel so that he could whisper in her ear. "Come on, baby, we love each other. Can't we work this out?"

"How can we work this out when you claim you want to marry me, but you also want an easy way out if you should ever change your mind? That's not the way it works with me. I have prayed for a forever kind of love, and I won't accept anything less."

Shaking his head, Dontae told her, "I don't ever plan to leave you." He averted his eyes a moment and then looked back at her and said, "But who knows, maybe one day you'll decide that you're not in love with me anymore... maybe you'll want to leave. Can you blame me for wanting to protect myself from that?"

"Yes," she said simply and then added. "I'm not going to say that you don't love me, because I believe that you do. But sometimes you are so distant that I don't even know how to reach you. Now if you can explain that to me, then maybe we have a shot."

When Dontae just stood there staring at her without opening his mouth to explain anything, Jewel said, "That's what I thought," and then walked away from him.

As Jewel and Dawn headed back to their room, Ronny turned to Dontae and asked, "So, does this mean the party is over?"

***

Carmella, Ramsey, Joy and Lance were all dressed up and seated at a table in the school gymnasium eating a chicken, rice and asparagus dinner that wasn't half bad. The dinner was in honor of Coach Linden and everyone seemed to be having a good time. Halfway through dinner, Lance leaned over to Joy and said, "The superintendent just walked in. I'm going to see if I can say hi."

"You go, boy, and bring back that contract so you can take me on that cruise you keep promising."

"You got it, babe." Lance leaned over and kissed Joy before he left the table.

As he walked away, Joy kept her eyes on her man. The love she had for her husband shone through her eyes as she smiled without even knowing that she was smiling.

"You can stop staring at him. I guarantee you that he'll be back," Carmella said as she nudged her daughter.

"I know, Mama. He's just so cute, I have a hard time keeping my eyes off of him," Joy said without an ounce of embarrassment.

Ramsey Sr. put his arms around Carmella as he told Joy. "I know exactly how you feel because I can't keep my eyes or hands off of your mother."

"TMI, okay... some things are just TMI." Joy put her hands over her ears as if she couldn't take hearing anymore.

"Oh please, you are a grown woman. And from the way you were just looking at your husband, I'd say that you know the deal," Carmella told her daughter.

"I'll never be grown enough to hear about my mother's love life."

"Okay, we'll leave you alone." Ramsey took his hand off of Carmella's shoulder and took the last bite of his chicken.

As the superintendent took the podium, Lance rushed back over to Joy and took his seat. "Did you miss me?"

"You know I did. I could hardly take my eyes off of you."

"That's enough, you two. If you don't want to hear my husband talk about our love life, I sure don't want to listen to the two of you fawning all over each other in public," Carmella said while giggling. She was actually ecstatic that Joy had finally found someone that she could love unconditionally. And she prayed that Dontae would soon come to terms with the love he had for Jewel and do whatever it took to hold onto that woman.

"It brings me great pleasure to introduce a great man... a man who has given of himself for over three decades... a man who has tirelessly worked to turn good players into great players." The superintendent stretched out his hand towards the coach and said, "My friend, Coach Linden."

Thunderous applause erupted throughout the room. Carmella stood and continued applauding the man who had helped her son break into the NFL. And then one by one people all over the room stood and gave Coach Linden the praise they thought he deserved.

Looking humbled by the applause, Coach Linden lowered his head in an aw-sucks kind of way. He then directed the crowd to take their seats. "Sit down, y'all. I am no one special. But I do thank you all for deciding to spend your evening with an old geezer like me."

The crowd erupted in laughter.

But just as Coach Linden was about to speak again, the double doors in the back of the gym swung open, banging loudly against the wall. Carmella and others turned in the direction of the noise and watched two police officers storm into the room. There was another man behind them. His face was filled with hatred as he yelled, "This man doesn't deserve to be honored for nothing."

The superintendent stood up and shouted, "What's going on here?"

"He raped my son," the angry man shouted back as he pointed to Coach Linden. "My boy trusted this monster and he took advantage of that trust."

The police officers were now standing on either side of Linden. The one with the handcuffs out said, "John Linden, You will need to come with us."

Linden didn't say a word as the handcuffs were placed on his wrists. The superintendent, though, was simply flabbergasted. He puffed out his cheeks as he demanded, "Uncuff him. We are having an awards banquet in his honor."

"Sorry Superintendent, you're going to have to find someone else to honor—because Coach Linden is on his way to a holding cell."

"Yeah! You're finally getting what's coming to your old lecherous self."

If Linden had looked humbled minutes before, he looked downright mortified now as the police officers escorted him out of the school building with the angry man screaming obscenities as he followed after them.

"What just happened here?" Joy asked as she looked around the table.

But Carmella wasn't so much worried about what had happened in the gym. She was more concerned with what might have happened ten years ago when Linden was Dontae's coach. Had she finally discovered the answer to why her son seemed so withdrawn and angry at times? She hoped to God that she hadn't.

6

Even though Dontae's weekend with Jewel had been a total bust, today was a good day, because his father had been released from prison. Dontae had driven from Charlotte to Raleigh to see him. His father hadn't wanted Dontae to pick him up at the prison site. He preferred catching the bus into town.

Dontae understood. Nelson Marshall had once been a powerful judge in the city of Raleigh. He'd had the goal of one day running for a seat in congress, but one affair had brought him low and he was now a slim measure of the man he once had been. Dontae had looked up to his father and feared his wrath. But today, he had come to restore some dignity back to the man who helped raise him.

Dontae had wanted his mom and sister to be with him when he met with his dad. He wanted them to see the look on Nelson Marshall's face the moment he realized that he didn't have to worry about starting over. But since they chose to go to Coach Linden's shame of an awards banquet last night, he really didn't want to talk to them right now.

Dontae pulled up at the Panera where he and his father had arranged to meet. He got out of his car, took a deep breath and then made his way into the bagel shop. His father hadn't been there for him at a time when he needed him the most, but Dontae was trying to forget about all of that now. His mother was always telling him that God gives out special blessings to people who stretch out their hand to give rather than to receive. Dontae was about to test out her theory.

Nelson was seated in a booth towards the back, waving like crazy as Dontae walked in. Dontae smiled and walked over to the booth. Nelson stood and hugged his son.

Dontae felt his eyes watering at his father's touch. He quickly pulled himself together, though, because they were surrounded by people and he didn't want anyone thinking he was soft, crying over a simple hug from his dad. Sitting down in the booth opposite Nelson, Dontae cleared his throat and said, "It's real good to see you."

Whereas Dontae was able to hold back his tears, Nelson just couldn't. He picked up a napkin and dabbed at his eyes. "Boy, you sure are a sight for these old eyes."

"You're not that old, Dad. You're still in your fifties."

"Yeah, well I'm closer to sixty than fifty and that's pretty old to be starting all over again." Nelson sighed, and then lifted his shoulders. "But I'm not concerned with that. I'm just thrilled to be home and to be able to see my family." With that said, Nelson dabbed at his eyes again.

"That's why I wanted to meet with you tonight, Dad... to let you know that you don't have to start from scratch." Dontae pulled an envelope out of his jacket pocket and handed it to his father.

"What's this?"

"Open it," was all Dontae said as an answer.

Nelson had this quizzical look on his face as he opened the envelope. As he pulled the contents out, Nelson's eyes widened and they filled with tears again. He looked like a broken man as he lowered his head and then passed the envelope back to Dontae. "I can't take this."

"Dad, what are you talking about? This is your money. I'm just giving it back to you."

Nelson looked up, hope springing forth. "What do you mean?"

"When you and mom divorced, you gave me the eighty thou you'd been saving for my college fund. But if you remember, I received a full scholarship, so I put the money in a CD and didn't touch it until yesterday when I cashed it in."

"But that check is for a hundred thousand."

"I made out pretty good on the interest," Dontae told his father as he handed back the check.

Nelson hesitated for a moment, but only a moment. He took the check and then asked, "Are you sure you want to do this? I know you received a scholarship, but I always assumed that you used the money for living expenses."

"Nope. Mama made me invest the money and wouldn't let me get an apartment with the money during my junior year when I wanted my own place." Dontae shrugged. "She was right, though. Because after busting up my knee, if I hadn't been able to keep most of my first year earnings, I would have needed that money real bad."

Nelson smiled then, but it was a bittersweet smile. "Your mom has always been the smartest woman I've ever met. And she can cook, too."

"The total package," Dontae said, not able to resist the urge to rub in that fact.

"Yeah, and I'm a total fool."

"You said it, I didn't." Dontae put his hand in front of his mouth to disguise the grin on his face.

"How are things going with you and Jewel?"

That wiped the grin off his face. Dontae said, "Not so good, Dad... like father like son, I guess."

Nelson shook his head, grief etched across his face. "Don't tell me you cheated on that woman?"

"No, nothing like that. She's just upset with me right now and I haven't been able to fix the situation yet." His phone beeped, letting him know that he had received a text. He looked at his phone. It was his mom asking him to call her. Dontae knew what she wanted to talk about, and he wasn't ready for that yet. So he ignored the text, just as he had ignored her calls earlier in the day.

"So where are you staying, Dad?"

"I'm at the Marriott down the street. Your sister booked me a room there for the week."

"So what's your plan after that?"

Nelson waved the envelope as he said, "This just made planning things a whole lot easier. I think I'll see if I can find a house to rent, one with a home office and then set out to find some consulting contracts."

"What kind of consulting will you be doing?"

Nelson had a light in his eyes as he spoke, "I thought about how I would build a career for myself every day that I spent behind bars. I worked in government all those years as a judge, so I know there is money to be made by helping businesses fill out government contracts. And with my law degree, I would also be able to review contracts for my clients."

"Sounds good, Dad. I'm glad you've got it all worked out."

"Now all we have to do is work out this situation you've gotten yourself into with Jewel," Nelson told his son.

***

"Don't you think you should give Dontae another chance?" Maxine, her oldest sister asked as she and Dawn hung out with her at an uptown eatery.

"You don't understand." Jewel took a sip of her iced tea and then said, "Dontae keeps part of himself hidden from me. I don't know from one day to the next who I'm going to be dealing with... the loving, attentive Dontae or the clouded and guarded Donate. He's got to change if he wants things to work between us and that's the bottom line."

"Okay, but you are going to lose that man if you don't hurry up and get over this attitude problem of yours," Maxine admonished.

Dawn shook her head. "I think you're wrong, Maxine." Dawn laid her fork on her plate. "I had been trying to get Jewel to work things out with Dontae also. I even tricked her into going out of town with me this past weekend so that Dontae could talk to her."

"You was wrong for that," Maxine said, laughing to herself about the things her sister had shared with her about their weekend adventure.

Dawn lifted her hands in surrender. "Okay, I was wrong. But I just wanted to help Jewel out... that is until I realized that she knows exactly what she's doing. Because I happen to believe that the divorce rate is as high as it is because people tend to look over the very things that bothered them about their mate even before they said, 'I do'."

Jewel nodded. "I have so many friends who have told me that they thought marriage would change their husband. So they put up with all his bad behavior until after the wedding. And all that did was cause more problems later on."

"Yeah, so leave her alone. Jewel knows what she needs from Dontae. And if he truly loves her like we think he does, then he's got to man up," Dawn said.

"Okay, you're right." Maxine put a hand on Jewel's shoulder. "We're here to support you, no matter what you decide to do."

But Jewel wasn't listening to anything her sisters had to say at the moment. Her concentration had been thrown off because of the picture of Dontae that had just flashed on the television screen above the bar area. She stood up and walked over to the bar as a close up of another male filled the screen. This man was in court being arraigned.

Jewel looked at the bartender as she pointed at the television and asked, "What's that about?"

The bartender looked up toward the television and said, "Oh, that's Coach Linden. He just got arrested for molesting the boys that he coached years ago."

"That's awful," Jewel said. "What school does he coach at?"

"He's a high school coach out of Raleigh."

Dontae grew up in Raleigh, was all Jewel could think as she went back to the table and grabbed her purse. "I've got to go," she told her sisters.

"What's wrong? You look like you just watched a murder or something," Dawn said.

"I need to call Dontae and make sure he's okay," was all she said as she left the restaurant.

***

Lance's cell phone was ringing. He sat up in bed and answered. Joy could only hear her husband's side of the conversation, but from what she could make out, the superintendent of schools was on the other end and Lance was arranging a meeting with the man.

When her husband hung up the phone, Joy said, "You're not still considering taking them on as a client, are you?"

"Why not?" Lance asked as he got out of bed, heading for the bathroom.

Joy jumped up. "That man might have done something to my brother, that's why."

"You don't know that for sure. Dontae hasn't said anything about Coach Linden," Lance said.

"We haven't talked to Dontae since Coach Linden got arrested the other night. So we can't confirm that Dontae wasn't one of his victims."

Lance lifted a hand. "*Alleged* victims."

"Don't you dare talk to me about being innocent until proven guilty." Joy was pacing the floor now. "And to think that I was against Dontae for being so rude to Coach Linden. But now I know why he didn't want to have anything to do with the man." She turned back to Lance. "And now my husband wants to represent that monster."

"Calm down, Joy."

"I'll calm down when you show some family loyalty. And it's not just Dontae that we need to be concerned with. Unless you've forgotten, my stepfather was the principal at that school for two years of the time that Coach Linden was there, so Ramsey could also be sued before all this is over."

Lance put his arm around his wife, trying to soothe her. "If I'm able to get these charges dropped, then nobody will be able to sue anybody."

Pushing her husband away from her, Joy asked, "What about my brother? If Coach Linden did something to him, shouldn't he be able to sue?"

Hunching his shoulders, Lance said, "I don't know what you want me to do."

Throwing up her hands, she turned away from him. "Go get in the shower and go to work, Lance. I don't even want to talk to you right now."

She sat back down on her bed and called her mother. When Carmella answered the phone she asked, "Have you talked to him?"

"I wish I had. But he's not returning my text messages or answering my calls."

"What are we going to do, Mom?"

"We're going to pray, and put this in God's hands. There is a reason why Dontae is avoiding us and it's all going to come to light."

Thinking about Lance representing the school against Coach Linden's victims put a knot in her stomach. "I really need to speak with him, Mom."

"Sunday is Mother's Day. Everyone else is going to be here, so I don't think Dontae is going to miss celebrating Mother's Day with me."

"Okay, so do you think we should ask him about this in front of the whole family?"

"We probably need to take him to the side, but let's pray about it."

"Okay Mom, I'll see you on Sunday. And hopefully we'll find out if Dontae is one of Coach Linden's victims."

"I hope not, Joy. Because if that is true, I just don't know what I'm going to do."

7

Carmella was having a banner day. Since she now had seven grown children with jobs, well... Ronny was between jobs, but Carmella believed that something was going to turn up for him soon. As far as Carmella was concerned, her heart was full because she would have six of her seven children in her home today. Rashan was still on the mission field and wouldn't be able to attend her Mother's Day brunch, but she and Ramsey had done Face Time with him earlier that morning.

Ramsey had somehow gotten all the men in the family to agree to cook the brunch. Carmella didn't have high hopes for the meal they were about to consume, but she would eat it with a smile on her face, just at the thought that the men in her life loved her enough to do this.

"I am so glad that we didn't have to slave in the kitchen today. It's about time the men do something productive around here," Renee said as she kicked her feet up on the lounge chair like the princess she thought she was.

"Since when have you ever slaved in the kitchen?" Raven scoffed at her sister's proclamation.

"I used to help Mom in the kitchen when we were kids all the time," Renee reminded her sister.

"You were Mom's little helper then," Raven agreed. "But you won't even come in the kitchen to help us now." Raven pointed towards Joy and Carmella when she said the word us.

Carmella saw the sad look on Renee's face and quickly came to her rescue. "Renee doesn't have to spend time with us in the kitchen. We spend time together other ways, don't we?"

Renee nodded and then as she looked intently at Carmella, she added, "But even though I don't cook with you... you do know that I love you, right?"

"I sure do, honey." Carmella reached over and gently touched Renee's arm. "And don't you ever feel bad for wanting to hold onto the memories you shared with your mother. Lord knows, I treasure every memory that I had with mine, and even though she's been gone from this earth for many, many years, there's still not a day that goes by that I don't wish she was here with me."

When Renee's eyes filled with tears, Joy, Carmella and Raven surrounded her and the four women group hugged. When the women parted, Renee wiped her eyes, shook her head as she mumbled, "Mother's Day... for the longest time, I didn't have anyone to spend this day with. But you know what?" she said while looking at Carmella. "If I can't spend this day with my birth mom, I sure am happy to be spending it with you."

"I understand exactly what you're going through," Joy told her. "It's kind of like how I felt at my wedding; I wanted my father to walk me down the aisle, but he was in jail. And then, Ramsey, being the wonderful step-father that he is, walked me down the aisle."

"Daddy was so proud. He told me that you were the first child he had the honor of walking down the aisle," Raven said.

"Don't get me wrong, Raven, I was truly grateful that Ramsey was there for me... but it didn't stop me from wishing it had been my dad."

"And I with you... with all of you," Carmella said as she kissed her girls' foreheads. Life was good, even when you had to struggle to get to the good part.

"Hey, what's going on in here?" Ramsey asked as he and the boys came out of the kitchen carrying plates and bowls of food.

Carmella glanced over at the men in her life. Ramsey was so open, honest and loving towards her. Ronny had a bright future in store, once he could figure out what the Lord put him on this earth to accomplish. Ramsey Jr. and Dontae already had their careers in order, but both men were nursing some wounds that were long overdue for healing. Ramsey had asked her to leave them alone. He said if they wanted to talk to their parents, they would come to them. Even though she mostly agreed with him, she couldn't allow Dontae to go another day without taking some of the burden off his shoulders.

Just as she was silently praying about how to approach the subject of Coach Linden—since it was obvious to everyone that Dontae did not want to talk about the man—the doorbell rang.

Carmella hopped up, thankful to have something to take her mind off of what she would have to do to her son before he walked away and just began ignoring their calls again. Looking out the peephole, Carmella was surprised to see Jewel on the other side. She had come to family events with Dontae before, but not since she and Dontae had broken up. *Lord, is this your answer to my prayers?*

Carmella swung open the door and said, "Bless the Lord, my son is going to be so happy to see you."

"Who is it, Mom?" Joy asked as she entered the foyer. When she saw Jewel, she began to smile. Joy hugged her and said, "I'm so glad you could make it."

"You knew she was coming?" Carmella asked with a puzzled look on her face.

Joy nodded and then whispered, "She's been trying to talk to Dontae about Coach Linden, too. I was hoping she could help us get some answers out of him."

"Dinner is on the table, so you two need to get back in there so we can eat and—" Dontae was saying as he entered the foyer. He stopped short as he caught sight of Jewel. "What are you doing here?"

"You haven't been answering my calls, and we need to talk," Jewel told him like a woman determined to get answers to mysteries that had troubled her for too long.

***

Looking at the women in his life, Dontae could see that each one of them wanted answers from him, but to give those answers he'd have to open himself up to things he didn't want to deal with or ever think about again. He put his hands in his pants pocket and felt his keys. "I'm going for a drive. Go ahead and eat without me."

"Don't do this, Dontae. Don't run out on the very people who love you and want to help you," his mother admonished.

"I'll be back. Just give me a little time to myself." He rushed out of the door before anyone could stop him. He just needed to get away. To be alone... to feel safe. But as he sped down the street his mind wouldn't let it go, wouldn't let him forget. So Dontae once again went back with that seventeen-year-old kid, away from home at a summer football camp. The football camp that Coach Linden had talked his parents into letting him attend. It had been ten years ago, but Dontae was reliving it as if it had just happened to him last night.

"Good game, boy. We are heading out of here with the championship and do you know who we have to thank for that?" Coach Linden strutted in front of the team like a man on his way to the Super Bowl. He answered his own question, "Our team MVP, Stevie Wallace and the boy wonder who scored the winning touchdown tonight, Dontae Marshall."

The locker room erupted in cheers.

Coach Linden then said, "So, you guys go on out and party and have yourselves a good time tonight. Be back by midnight." He held up a room key. "And Dontae and Stevie get to stay in the suite tonight. There's two bedrooms and plenty of room in the living area to throw another party."

All smiles, Stevie grabbed the room key with excitement dancing in his eyes. "Thanks, coach." Stevie turned to Dontae and said, "We're picking up some girls tonight."

Dontae smiled, thinking that he was about to score and Coach Linden had made it all possible. The boy hung out, getting a little rowdy at times, but mostly just having fun and celebrating their win. Their fake ID's weren't working, so a bunch of them decided to go back to the hotel and get into the liquor that Coach Linden had stashed in the suite that Stevie and Dontae would be staying in. They ran into a few girls who wanted to hang out with them, so they all went back and got their party started with booze and music and dancing.

Around midnight Coach Linden opened the door and came into the suite. He turned off the music. Everyone turned and stared at him. His hands were on his hips and smoke was coming out of his nose as he yelled, "Do you know how many complaints I have received about all the loud music coming out of this room?"

"But coach, we were just having fun like you told us to," Brad, one of the football players said.

"I didn't tell you all to disturb the entire hotel." Coach Linden pointed towards the door. "Party over, get to your rooms."

"What about us, coach? Do we still get to sleep here tonight?" Stevie half asked and half slurred because he had drunk more than his fair share of the booze.

"You and Dontae can stay, but it's lights out for everyone." He pointed at the girls. "I'll call you a cab, so that you can get home safely."

Feeling ill from all the beer he'd drunk through the night, Dontae was ready to lay it down. He went to his room, closed the door, took off his jeans and threw them on the floor. He didn't have the energy to do anything else, so Dontae fell face first onto the bed. He heard himself snoring as his head hit the pillow.

Dontae didn't know how long he had slept before he felt someone lying in the bed with him. At first Dontae thought he was dreaming and imagined that one of the girls from the party had snuck into his room. But even in his drunken state, something didn't feel right. The hand that was moving down his back and then touching other parts of his body didn't seem girly. It was more like the touch of big, clumsy man hands. Dontae jumped out of bed and fumbled around in the dark until he found the light switch. Coach Linden was lying in his bed naked and smiling up at him.

"What are you doing? Get out of my bed," Dontae said in a low voice. He wanted to yell at his coach, but

Stevie was in the next room and he didn't want anyone to know what Coach Linden had just tried to pull.

"What wrong?" Coach Linden asked. "I just wanted to sleep in here with you tonight."

Coach Linden was married. Dontae never imagined that the man was gay. But the world was full of people who went both ways... maybe that was how Coach Linden lived his life. But Dontae's parents had brought him up in church and had taught him right from wrong. They'd opened the Bible to the book of Romans and showed him where God spoke of men and women who became lovers of their own kind, and how the word of God said such acts were unseemly and would be judged by God.

"You'll have to kill me before I get back in that bed with you," Dontae told him and prepared to fight to the death. But then his stomach lurched and the illness he felt earlier erupted as he vomited all over himself and the floor.

"Clean yourself up," Linden growled as he got off the bed and pulled the boxers he'd left on the side of the bed back on. He flung open the door and stormed out of the room, looking as if Dontae disgusted him. Dontae ran over to the door, quickly closed and locked it. Looking down at his shirt, Dontae saw clumps of vomit splattered over it. He wanted to go and wash himself off, but the bathroom was across the hall and he'd left his duffle bag full of clothes in the living room; there was no way he was going out there tonight.

Dontae took his shirt off, wiped his mouth and neck with it and then threw it on the floor. Looking at the bed where Coach Linden had been laying with him made Dontae feel ill again. He couldn't get back in that bed. He wanted to call his dad to find out what he should do. After all, his dad was a big time judge; he'd know how to fix Coach Linden. But it was too late to call his house. The team was heading home in the morning, so he would just tell his dad what happened when he got home.

Dontae pulled the blanket off the bed and sat down in the chair across from the bed, put the cover around him and slept off and on. Every time he thought he heard a noise, he would jump and try to keep his eyes open, until his lids would close on their own.

By morning Dontae's eyes were red and sleep deprived, but he didn't care. He'd made it through the night without Coach Linden coming back to his door. Now he just needed to get on that plane and get home. Someone knocked on his door and Dontae practically jumped out of his skin and then shouted, "Go away."

"I'm leaving your duffle bag in front of the door. Get dressed so we can all get to the airport on time," Coach Linden said through the door.

It took Dontae five minutes to gather up enough nerve to open the door to get his duffle. But the simple fact that he couldn't go home until he got dressed and left this hotel room was the one thing that set a fire under him. Coach Linden wasn't standing at the door waiting to pounce on *him, so he pulled his bag into the room and quickly got dressed. Throwing the bag's strap over his shoulder, Dontae rushed out of the hotel room and made his way to the lobby where some of the other team members were already waiting. He hadn't thought about Stevie at all that morning. Not until he saw him walking towards them and noticed that Stevie wouldn't make eye contact with him. At that moment, Dontae realized that after leaving his room, Coach Linden must have snuck into Stevie's room.*

When Dontae had made it home, he'd discovered that his father had left his mother for another woman. The following week, Stevie dropped out of school and tried to commit suicide. Everyone assumed that the anger Dontae displayed when he came back from camp stemmed from his parents' break-up, but year after year as he'd kept Coach Linden's secret, Dontae felt as if he was, in effect, sending that monster to the more defenseless Stevie's room.

Now his family wanted answers, but how could he tell them that it wasn't just what Coach Linden did to him that ate at him, but the fact that he hadn't yelled out that night and exposed Coach Linden. If Dontae had run into the room that night, maybe Coach Linden would have been too ashamed at being caught to try the same thing with Stevie, who had been so wasted that he probably hadn't been able to fend the man off.

8

"I'm worried, Mama. Do you think I made a mistake by inviting Jewel? Maybe, Dontae won't come back because he wouldn't want her to hear what he has to say." Joy was wringing her hands as she stood next to her mother.

Carmella shook her head as she exhaled. "If he's going to marry that girl, he owes her the whole truth and nothing but the truth. Time out for married couples keeping secrets from their spouses."

"Amen to that," Joy said and then added. "I wish you would say that to my husband."

Carmella looked concerned as she asked, "Has Lance been keeping secrets from you? Is something going on with you and Lance? Is that why he's not here today?"

"He's celebrating Mother's Day with his own mother today. But you're right, there is something between us."

Brunch had been eaten an hour ago, now everyone was in the family room watching television while Joy and Carmella hung out in the kitchen. Carmella sat down on the stool next to her daughter. "What's wrong?" She held her breath, praying that whatever it was, it was something that could be fixed.

"Lance has been meeting with the school board. He's very close to striking a deal to represent them."

"But isn't that what you wanted? You asked me to attend that awards banquet on Lance's behalf, remember. You told me that he wanted to become the lawyer of record for the school systems," Carmella reminded Joy.

Joy hung her head in misery. She couldn't decide what was more important in this instance... loyalty to her husband or to her brother. "It's just that with the way Dontae has been acting, I truly believe that Coach Linden did something to him. So, I think Lance should stick by his family and not represent people who have brought harm to us."

Carmella rubbed Joy's back. "I can understand how you feel. But whether Lance decides to represent them or not, he's still the man you fell in love with and he's still the man you promised to spend the rest of your life with. So your job is to love him, even when you don't agree with him."

"I don't know if I can do that in this situation, Mom."

"Then you had no business getting married. He's your husband, Joy. Stand by him."

"How can you ask me to do that? That coach may have done something despicable to your son and you want me to stand by my husband if he decides to represent those people for his own selfish reasons?"

Carmella pointed at her chest. "I can be mad at Lance all I want to be. But I will not ask you to bear my burden. You took vows with your husband before God. Just because the road gets a little rough, that doesn't change the promises you made."

Joy wanted to argue her point, but she knew she'd never win this argument with Carmella Marshall-Thomas. So she simply said, "Mama, sometimes I think you are just too saved for your own good."

Carmella shook her head. "You can never be too saved." She stood and said, "Come on, let's get back in the family room with the rest of the family."

Nodding as if she was coming to terms with something, Joy stood and followed her mother. But just as they were rounding the corner for the family room, the front door opened and Dontae walked in with Nelson following behind.

Stepping towards his mom, Dontae said, "I'm only telling this story once, so Dad stays or no go."

Carmella looked at Nelson. She had spent twenty-three years of her life with him. During those years of her marriage, Nelson had seemed little "g" godlike to her. He had been a wonderful provider and a great father to his children. She never dreamed that Nelson would cheat on her and had been caught off guard and thrown for several loops when she discovered the truth. But that was then and this was now. The man standing before her now had been humbled by life and the mistakes that he'd made; she could see the difference in him by the sadness in his eyes and the slight slump of his shoulders. "You're welcome to stay, Nelson. How have things been going?"

He stepped forward. "I'm looking for an apartment and making contacts so that I can get my life back on track."

"I've been praying for you. And if your children have anything to say about it, you'll be back on track before you know it."

Joy hugged her daddy. "I was going to stop by the hotel to check on you tonight, but I'm glad you're here with us now."

They went into the family room. Dontae rushed over to Jewel and took her hand. "I'm glad you're still here."

"I wanted to wait for you. I knew you'd come back." She gave him a weak smile and squeezed his hand.

Carmella whispered in Ramsey's ear and he nodded, then got up and shook Nelson's hand. "Good to have you back home. The kids have missed you."

"I missed them something awful as well," Nelson said and then added, "And thank you for allowing me to come in here so I can hear what my boy has to say."

"Not a problem." Ramsey turned to Dontae. "Do you want me to clear the room so you can talk with your mom and dad in private?"

Dontae shook his head. "You're all my family. I've been holding this in so long that I just want to say it once and be done with it."

"All right, in that case, the floor is yours," Ramsey said before sitting back down next to Carmella.

Dontae glanced around the room. One by one he took in the faces of his brothers and sisters, his parents and then Jewel. He studied her face the longest because he wanted to know if she would look at him differently after he opened himself up and exposed his wounds. There might not be a need for a prenup at all after this day was over, because Jewel might just decide she didn't want to marry someone like him.

Dontae knew that he wouldn't be able to tell his story if he kept looking at Jewel, so he turned to safer territory. He looked at his mom as he opened his mouth and confessed everything that happened that last night at football camp. He finished up by telling them about Stevie. To Dontae's surprise, he told his story with dry eyes. The tears hadn't come until he started thinking about Stevie again.

Carmella quickly came to his side. "It's not your fault, Dontae. Don't torment yourself like this."

"You don't understand, Mama. If I would have hollered and even tried to alert Stevie to what Coach

Linden tried to pull with me, then he might not have gone into Stevie's room that night and Stevie would have kept playing ball and he certainly would have been recruited before me. He was just that good."

"You were victimized by Coach Linden, Dontae. Most victims don't holler out, or tell anyone what their victimizer is doing." Renee stood up and went to Dontae also. "When I was in the eighth grade a girl bullied me unmercifully. But it wasn't until the end of the school year that I finally confess to Dad what I was going through. That's why I work as a youth counselor now. I want to give kids a place to turn, when they think there is nowhere to turn."

Dontae leaned on Renee's shoulder and cried through his sorrows. He wished he'd had someone like his little sister in his life back then. But then his mother started crying and Dontae turned from his little sister and took his mother in his arms and tried to soothe her pain.

The entire time Dontae was telling his story, Nelson had been like a ticking time bomb. He'd held his peace so that Dontae would be able to get everything out that was bothering him, but he could take it no more. He stood with fists clenched. "I'm going to kill him."

Joy put her hand on her father's shoulder and said, "You just got out of jail, Dad. We can't have you going back so soon. I'm going to kill him. And then maybe my husband won't have to decide who to represent."

The rest of the evening turned into an, I'm-mad-as-H-E-L-L-and-I'm-not-going-to-take-it-anymore episode. The men were all ready to ride out. They wanted to go bail Coach Linden out of jail and then drive him to a wooded area, let him out of the car and then hunt him down. They'd tie him to a tree and whip him until he begged for his life. Then they would just go on and kill him anyway.

The women's thoughts weren't any better. Instead of tying the man to a tree, they wanted to string him up by his toes, let him hang there while they took turns stabbing him in the heart. For what else would you do with a monster, but drive something through his black heart?

A house full of Christians and nobody thought to pray, not that night anyway. The wound was too fresh and too devastating. Tears brought them comfort and anger and thoughts of revenge became their friend.

Once things had quieted down in the house, Dontae and Jewel went out on the porch and sat for a while. When he finally mustered up enough nerve to look at her again, he was thankful that he didn't see anything different in her eyes. But he had to hear her say it. "So, I guess you're thanking God that you gave me back that ring now, huh?"

"Why would you think something like that?"

"Well, now you know why I'm so messed up in the head."

"If I'm thanking God about anything, it's that you made it through the horrific part of your life and that I now know you a little bit better." She put her hand over his and looked at him with compassion showing on her face. "Thank you for sharing that with me."

Dontae poked himself in the head several times. "I just wish I could get it out of my head. I've been so angry for so long that I just want it all to stop."

"You know how the Bible tells us that God casts our sins into the sea and remembers them no more?"

"Yeah," Dontae answered wondering what that had to do with what Coach Linden did to him and to Stevie and to countless others.

"I sometimes wish that we could cast the sins that people do to us in some sea of forgetfulness and that way we wouldn't have to ever give them the satisfaction of thinking about them anymore."

"Yeah, me too," Dontae said as he looked off into nothingness. The street was dark now and it was getting late. With the two hour drive he had ahead of him, he would have normally been gone by now. He noticed Jewel's car parked across the street. "You don't plan to drive back tonight do you?"

"I hadn't planned on staying so late. I'm on a deadline and need to get back to work."

"You work from home, so there's no need for you to get on the road tonight." He turned to her. "Look, just stay here with my parents; I'll bunk with my dad for the night and then I'll follow you back to Charlotte in the morning, okay?"

Hesitating for a moment, she finally said, "I can see that you're worried about me. And you already have enough on your mind, so I won't get on the highway tonight. I'll wait and drive back with you in the morning."

"Thank you." He lifted her hand and kissed it. "I wanted to tell you about all of this a while ago, but I kept worrying that you'd think that I was gay or something and then not want to be with me."

Shaking her head, Jewel put her hands on his face and gently told him, "You are not what was done to you. Don't confuse the two. An evil monster molested you, that doesn't make you gay... just makes you a victim."

"I don't like thinking of myself as a victim."

"Nobody does." She kissed his forehead as she said, "But as long as evil is in this world, there will always be a monster out there victimizing someone."

"I think I managed to convince myself that since he didn't do anything but touch me, I hadn't been molested. But you're right, that's exactly what he did to me."

"What he tried to do was steal your future. But look at you, Dontae you made it, despite what Coach Linden did. You beat him; don't you know that?"

Dontae stood, walked to the edge of the porch and then turned back to face her. "To tell you the truth, I'm not sure what I believe right now. I just know that I need you in my life... I need your love."

"You never have to doubt my love for you, Dontae."

Looking at her ring finger he asked, "Then why aren't you wearing my ring?"

"I want to wear it," she admitted with surprising ease. "But I don't think you're ready for a lifelong commitment yet. But when you are, please come find me. I'll be waiting." With that she stood up and went back inside the house.

Dontae wanted to go after her and deny her assertion about his marriage readiness. But deep down he knew she was right. She had him pegged. Something was holding him back and he would be spending the night with that person, so maybe he'd try to figure some things out about himself.

***

At the hotel with his dad, they both tried to put up a front like everything was normal between them. But as Dontae lay on one double bed and his father on the other, they both knew it wasn't true. Nothing would ever be normal between them again, but they could still move forward in this new normal that they would somehow create.

Dontae turned to his father and asked, "So Dad, how did you like being at the house tonight with mom and her new family?"

Nelson had no words, just shook his head.

But Dontae saw the regret in his eyes. "Why couldn't you make it work with , Mom? I don't understand how Jasmine got to you in the first place."

"I had lost my way, I guess. In pursuit of my career, I had stopped going to church on a regular basis and just became consumed with what I wanted and I wasn't thinking about what was best for my family. Cheating became easy after that."

They were silent for a long while after Nelson's confession then Nelson asked, "Why didn't you tell me about Coach Linden trying to make a move on you?"

"I wanted to. The whole ride home all I could think about was how powerful my dad was and how you would make Coach Linden pay for what he'd done to me and Stevie. But when I got home everything had changed. Mom was falling apart and was trying desperately to pick the pieces of her life back up and you had moved on with Jasmine. You didn't have time for me anymore."

"And then I let Jasmine call the police on you, so you thought that I wouldn't hear anything you had to say, huh?"

Dontae nodded.

Nelson found that he hadn't shed the last tears over how much his affair had cost his family. He'd lost a career, done prison time and almost destroyed his family. And for what? Some woman who wasn't even in his life anymore, nor did he want her in his life, for that matter. "I'm sorry, son. I'm so sorry. All I can do is promise to be there for you from now on. I'm going to make this up to you... you have my word."

"That's all I need, Dad. Now stop crying and get some sleep." Dontae hit his pillow to fluff it up a bit so he could get a good night's rest. He was drained from having to comfort his mother earlier and now watching his dad fall apart over his revelation was just too exhausting. "This has got to be the worst Mother's Day Mom has ever had."

"Without a doubt," Nelson agreed while wiping the tears from his face. "But at least she had Ramsey to help her get through this."

9

Three days had passed since Dontae had told them what Coach Linden tried to do to him. Like the others, Carmella hadn't taken it well. But unlike the others, Dontae was her son, and it felt as if her heart was bleeding. She hadn't gone in to work on Monday or Tuesday. That morning, Ramsey had gone in to do the bookkeeping for her while her clerks handled the baking.

But now it appeared as though Ramsey had had enough of her moping around the house. He stood at the end of the bed with hands fisted on his hips. "How much longer, Carmella?"

Playing dumb she asked, "How much longer, what?"

"A few of the kids called me this afternoon. They're worried about you because they haven't received the Praise Alert you normally email out to them."

Guilt crossed her face. "I forgot to send that out." She sunk further into her pillow. "Would you mind scouring the internet to find a praise report for me and then send it to the kids?"

Sitting down on the bed next to his wife, Ramsey gently told her, "I can do a lot of things to help you get through this difficult time. I can hold your hand, love you... I can even go down to the bakery and help the staff make those scrumptious desserts that you are so famous for. But I cannot praise the Lord for you. That's an individual thing and something you will have to do on your own."

Tears flowed down Carmella's face as she accepted Ramsey's word as truth. God would not settle for a substitute praiser. Everyone must give God His due out of their own hearts. But right now Carmella's heart was so heavy, and she was so ashamed at the condition she'd found herself in that she didn't even feel worthy to praise God.

Ramsey lifted her into his arms and held onto her. "Dontae is all right, baby. He survived. The enemy didn't tear him down, so don't let it tear you down."

"I was supposed to protect Dontae, and I allowed him to go somewhere with that monster."

"I was Dontae's principal at the time, and I hadn't recognized what was going on. And evidently, Coach Linden was doing all this right under my nose."

"But I'm Dontae's mother, I should have paid more attention to what was going on."

Ramsey shook his head. "You didn't know, Carmella. This is not your fault and I'm not going to sit here and let you carry this all on your shoulders. The blame and the shame belong to Linden and Linden alone."

"You just don't understand, Ramsey. None of this was ever supposed to happen. Grown men aren't supposed to molest teenage boys." She put her hand to her heart as the tears kept coming and said, "And now I feel so much hatred in my heart towards Coach Linden that it scares me."

"It happens, Carmella. I was so livid when I found out about Renee getting bullied for an entire year that I wanted to hurt that kid."

"I've never felt like this before, Ramsey. Not even when Nelson and Jasmine were sending me through all kinds of drama, never once did I feel hatred towards them. But I am feeling so much hatred for Coach Linden right now that I don't even know... how can I praise God when I'm feeling like this?"

Ramsey held on tighter, as he told his wife, "You praise Him anyhow. Isn't that what you've always told me? Through the pain, through the grief and even through the hatred. You keep praising God until He moves the thing that is hindering you out of the way."

***

On her knees, with hands steepled, Jewel cried out to the God she had known since she was fifteen and called out to Him in the back of her grandmother's church, asking Him to come into her heart. Since that day, Jewel had always trusted that God would look out for her and make her into who He wanted her to be. She believed that God was powerful enough to bring the man of her dreams into her life and that He was able to keep them together. Today she was adding something else to the things she believed God was well able to do.

"Thank You, Father, for always being here for me. I thank you for keeping me and for blessing me over and over again. You've even blessed me with things that I don't know about. Things that I don't readily see... so I just want to thank You for everything. Because I know that if anything good has ever come into my life, You were right in the midst of it.

"Dontae was one of those good things that You sent my way. I know we've had our differences lately, but that's only because I'm trying to get him to understand this concept of forever love the way You have shown it to me. But in the meantime, Lord Jesus, I'm asking you for a special blessing for Dontae. I'm asking that You renew his mind and even erase part of it. Make it so that he is able to forget the man who tried to destroy his life, even forget the very act. I believe you can do this, Lord God, and I will keep praying this prayer until the day it manifests for

Dontae. Thank You, in Jesus' mighty, can-do-anything-but-fail, name I pray this prayer."

***

"Welcome to my humble abode," Dontae said as he opened the door to let his father into his home. Nelson had called at about seven in the morning and asked Dontae to stay home from work that day. "So, I guess you're ready to tell me why you decided to drive all the way to Charlotte and why I had to take the day off of work?"

"I came to see my favorite son," Nelson told him as he walked in, looking around the house.

"Funny... I'm your only son." Dontae stopped, thought about it for a minute and then said, "At least I thought I was your only son. But feel free to correct me if I'm wrong."

Nelson slapped Dontae on the back. "You thought right. I was just joking with you."

"Are you hungry?" Dontae asked as he headed to the fridge.

"Naw, I picked up a breakfast sandwich on the way down." Nelson sat down on the stool in front of the kitchen island. "Where are your step-brothers?"

Dontae took out a jug of orange juice, poured it in a glass and took a sip. "Ramsey's at work and Ronny is out picking up some material for this new business he's all excited about starting."

"Oh really, what's he working on?"

Putting the jug of juice back in the fridge, Dontae said, "He won't say. Claims he wants to present it to us once he has everything in order."

"I hope it works out for him."

"If this doesn't, something will. Ronny is destined for success, just needs the right project."

"I'm searching for the right project myself... can't see myself going back into law. But this old dog still has a few tricks left."

"You'll find something, Dad. I have faith in you."

"Well, one thing is for sure; I still have connections. And those connections have brought me to your door this morning."

Dontae sat down with his father. "What's up?"

"I found Stevie Wallace."

Dontae looked at his father like he had grown two heads. "Why were you looking for Stevie?"

Nelson put his hand on Dontae's shoulder. "Listen to me for a minute, son." Dontae nodded, giving his father the floor, Nelson continued, "When I was in prison, I sat in my cell every night thinking about one thing and one thing only... redemption. I told God that if He would give me another chance, I would never neglect my family again in life. And God has given me another chance with you and your sister and I'm so thankful for that."

"What does Stevie have to do with you receiving redemption?" Dontae asked.

Nelson's throat was getting dry. "Can I get a bottle of water?"

"Sure thing, Dad." Dontae hopped up and grabbed a bottle of water from the cabinet below the sink. He handed it to his father and sat back down.

"I know you contacted the DA and agreed to testify against Coach Linden, and I think that's a good step forward. Putting Coach Linden away will stop him from hurting any more kids that have been placed in his care. But Stevie... that's where your redemption lies."

Dontae was silent as he thought about what his father was saying to him. In a way it made sense. He had always felt guilty for not warning Stevie about Coach Linden and for not helping him while he was being attacked. That night, he'd denied himself the knowledge of what was going on in the next room. Because if he had acknowledged that the sounds were Stevie calling out for help, then he would've had to do something. And Dontae had just gone to sleep, hoping that he, himself would not be further victimized that night.

Dontae had avoided thinking about Stevie for so many years, but indirectly, Stevie had always been on his mind. He saw him in every young recruit with all the potential in the world that he signed to his agency. Dontae guarded his clients and shielded them from the things in the sports industry that could do them harm. He had taken to his career change like a fish to water, because with each new recruit, he had been subconsciously looking out for Stevie.

Now it was time for him to look Stevie Wallace in the face and go hard for the redemption he now needed so desperately.

"Maybe you're right this time. It's way past time for me to man-up and face Stevie."

Nelson stood, pulled his keys out of his pocket. "Let's go."

Dontae hesitated. "You want to go right... right now? How do you even know where Stevie is?"

"When you mentioned that Stevie had been arrested, I figured he might be in jail right now or at least on parole. So, I made a few calls and found out that he's been out for about six years and has kept his nose clean. He's married with three kids, but because of the felony on his record Stevie has been bouncing around from job to job. He's working at a gas station in South Carolina, just fifteen minutes away from your house."

When Dontae first moved on the southwest part of Charlotte, he'd thought it strange how he could be driving down the street and be in North Carolina one moment but then in South Caroline the next. The two states probably needed to drop the whole 'north' and 'south' business and just go on and be plain old Carolina. But he wasn't in government, so he wasn't going to tell them how to run their business. And anyway, he had bigger things to concern himself with, at least that's the way Dontae saw it. "You took the time to find all of that out?"

Nelson nodded and then said, "The way I see it, your mom made out pretty good when she married Ramsey. He's a good guy and I'm glad that she's happy. But I'm still your and Joy's daddy, so it's my job to take care of you two."

"Some more of that redemption, Dad?"

"Yeah." Nelson shook his keys and then said, "Now, let's go get you some redemption."

Dontae had seen the gas station numerous times as he drove down this street, but he'd never pulled in. It was one of those mom and pop service stations that also did car repairs. He got out of the car, looked back and noticed that his dad was still in the driver's seat. He started to say something, but then Nelson lowered the passenger window and said, "Go on. I'll be right here when you get back."

Squaring his shoulders, Dontae pulled up his big-boy britches and walked into the gas station to handle his business. No customers were inside and no one was behind the counter. There was a note taped to the counter that encouraged customers to tap on a small bell for service. Dontae figured that they probably didn't have a lot of customers, so they were able to run the shop with one clerk at a time. He tapped the bell and waited.

"I'm coming."

Dontae heard the deep baritone voice and immediately recognized it from back in the day when Stevie had the ball in his hand and was headed down the field shouting, "check him, check him" or "I got this" and then, "touchdown".

Stevie stepped into the business area of the gas station. He was wearing overalls and wiping some black substance from his hands that Dontae assumed was oil. He hadn't seen Stevie since high school, so he still remembered him as the touchdown-kid. But Stevie wasn't just a scorer, he had an uncanny ability to read his opponents. He could spot their weaknesses and their strengths and he'd use them to get inside their heads.

"What can I do for you?" Stevie asked without looking up.

Dontae waited. He wanted to gauge Stevie's reaction once he realized who was standing in his place of business. Dontae didn't have to wait long. Stevie put the rag down and glanced up. He did a double take. His face went through several different emotions and then he held out his hand. "Dontae Marshall, how've you been?"

"Some days good." Dontae shrugged. "Others, not so good."

Stevie acknowledged that he understood how Dontae was feeling with a head nod. "I watched the game that night. I felt like it was me they were pulling off the field."

"I got through it," Dontae said as he held his chin up like a boy who'd been told, after scraping his knee, that a man has to be strong.

"So what brings you here?" Stevie asked.

Now that he was there looking Stevie in the face, Dontae was struggling with how to best approach the topic. He tossed a couple conversation starters around in his head and then finally landed on, "I just wanted you to know that I'm going to be testifying against Coach Linden when his case comes up."

"Good for you," Stevie said as if he couldn't care less. He picked the rag he'd been wiping his hands with back up and said, "I need to get back to work."

Dontae tried another approach. "Look, if you don't want me to mention your name, I won't."

He averted his eyes as he said, "Why would you mention my name in association with Coach Linden?"

Dontae was taken aback by the way Stevie was playing this. He never expected Stevie to deny that anything ever happened. "Stevie, I was there, remember? Coach Linden tried to attack me first."

"It was nice seeing you, Dontae." Stevie started walking away.

Dontae reached into his jacket pocket and pulled out a business card. "Take this." He handed Stevie the card. "I'm in Charlotte now, so if you ever want to talk, I will make myself available to you."

Stevie nodded as he put the card in his pocket and then headed back to work.

"How did it go?" Marshall asked when Dontae got back in the car.

Dontae shrugged. "Not really sure. He pretended like nothing happened. I got the impression real quick that he wanted to be anywhere but in that small space with me, so I gave him my business card and told him to get in touch if he ever wanted to talk."

"Well, that's all you can do then. Now, hopefully, you can put everything about Linden out of your mind," Nelson said as he drove his son down the street.

"That's one thing that I can't do." Dontae pointed at his head. "As hard as I try, I just can't get it out of my mind."

10

While Dontae was trying to figure out how to get things out of his mind that never should have been there in the first place, Joy was on the phone with Jewel trying to get her to accept Dontae just the way he was. "You know, when you love someone, you sometimes have to put up with things you wouldn't normally put up with," Joy said as she watched Lance stroll into the kitchen and pour himself a cup of coffee.

"I know, Joy. And I truly do love Dontae, but I don't want to help him get into something that he might later regret getting into."

"Dontae would never regret marrying you. And I promise that I will stop butting into his business if you will just take that ring back." Joy prayed that Dontae would never find out that she made this call. But even though they were both grown, she was still his big sister and felt an obligation to look out for him.

Joy had no idea what had been tormenting Dontae all these years. She thought all of his issues stemmed from their parents divorcing after twenty-three years of marriage. But clearly, Dontae had been battling a different demon altogether. Joy had been the one to invite Jewel to her mother's house on Mother's Day, so if the fallout from that day caused Dontae and Jewel to drift further apart, she'd never forgive herself.

"I am here for Dontae. He knows that. I just don't think we should be making wedding plans at a time when he needs to be dealing with other issues."

Lance was leaning against the kitchen counter, sipping his coffee and staring at her. Joy conceded. "Okay, I'll give you that. But as long as I know that you're still in Dontae's corner, then I'm satisfied with that. And I'll get out of your business."

"I know that you're just looking out for your brother, so I'm not offended or anything. You can call me any time," Jewel told her.

Joy thanked her for understanding and then hung up.

"It really does mean a lot to you, doesn't it, babe?" Lance asked as he set his mug down and approached his wife.

"What means a lot to me?" Joy had been trying her level best to do as her mother instructed her. But having just hung up with the love of Dontae's life and accepting the fact that the wedding was, at best, postponed, she really didn't know if she could do this stand-by-your-man stuff right now... especially if he was about to start up another conversation about that case.

"That we be supportive of Dontae." He was only a whisper's distance from her now.

How should she take his question? Was he finally hearing her or was he just going to start another debate? She didn't have the energy to try to figure her husband out, so she just decided to go with the truth. "Dontae is important to me. So, yeah, it's also important that I support him, especially in light of what he went through, and what so many others had to endure at the hand of Coach Linden."

Lance put his wife's hand in his. "I've done a lot of soul searching this week."

"Oh yeah?" was all she said to that.

"I had to ask myself if my ambitions were more important to me than my family. And do you know what I decided?"

She couldn't get the lump out of her throat so she could speak. Joy was terrified of the answer, because in that moment she would discover if her husband loved her enough to do something that would cost him dearly, career-wise. She well knew that the exposure that this court case would receive alone, would give Lance more notoriety than he'd ever had on any case before. Could he walk away from that for her?

"When I married you," Lance began, "I knew that I would have to give up certain cases because you're a prosecutor and I couldn't agree to defend anyone who you were prosecuting. But it never entered my mind that I might also have to give up cases that our family members might be involved in."

She leaned in and touched her forehead to his. "I never thought we'd have to face a situation like this either. I'm sorry if I've been difficult to deal with these past few weeks."

"Thank you for saying that." He kissed her forehead. "But you were right. The superintendent wasn't all that excited about me until he realized that Ramsey was my father-in-law and Dontae my brother-in-law. I don't even think they knew about what Coach Linden had done to Dontae, because they wanted me to get Dontae to be a character witness for Linden. I laughed in their faces at that."

"No honey, you didn't laugh in their faces. That's not professional at all," Joy said, but she was thrilled that Lance had too much integrity to approach Dontae with something like that.

"I didn't have to worry about being professional with them, because I told them that I couldn't take the case."

She screamed. "I am so happy right now. Thank you, Lance. You don't know how much this means to me."

"I hope it means a whole lot, because my earning potential just got a bit lighter."

"Oh ye of little faith. The God I serve knows how to reward us for unselfish acts of kindness," Joy told him before wrapping her arms around him and thoroughly kissing him.

***

Dontae was in his office reviewing some contracts when he received a call from Ronny. "What's up?" Dontae asked when he picked up the phone.

"I know you're busy so I'm not going to hold you, but I was just wondering if you'd noticed that we didn't receive a Praise Alert from Mama Carmella last week or this week either."

Dontae had noticed, but he didn't want to say anything, because his mom was probably still upset over his confession and needed a little break. The Thomas men hadn't been around when Carmella Marshall had fallen apart after his father asked for a divorce. But Dontae had. And he'd witnessed his mother lean on God for the strength to pick herself back up. She would be all right. "Do you think we should head to Raleigh to check on her this weekend?"

"I'm going to call Dad and see what's going on. We might need to ride out though. Ramsey's been tripping over it, too. We need those inspirational stories. Mama Carmella can't just quit on us."

"I hear you."

"Well, get back to work. I'll let you know what I find out after I talk to Dad."

"All right. I'll be home late tonight. Jewel wants me to take her to that new Tyler Perry movie."

"Why don't you call Dawn? I wouldn't mind double dating."

Dontae laughed. "Thanks anyway, bro. But I got this." They hung up and Dontae continued reviewing the contracts for his clients.

Around three in the afternoon, his assistant buzzed him. "A Mr. Steven Wallace is here to see you. He doesn't have an appointment, but he assured me that you will see him."

Dontae jumped out of his seat. "Send him in."

It had been a couple of weeks since Dontae saw Stevie, but as he walked into his office, Dontae noticed that he had on the same greasy overalls he'd had on the day Dontae visited him. "Good to see you, Stevie. What brings you on this side of town?"

Stevie plopped down in the chair in front of Dontae's desk. "I got fired today. Business is slow, so as usual, I had to go."

"I'm sorry to hear that."

Stevie waved Dontae's concern away. "I'll find another job. Might even start my own lawn care business or something."

Dontae was reminded of his father saying that Stevie had a hard time holding onto a job due to the felony on his record. Dontae found himself thinking, *But for the grace of God, there go I.*

"I sat in my car for about an hour having a real pity party about my lot in life. I felt awful about losing another job and didn't know how I was going to tell my wife. But then I thought about a time when I felt worse... much worse and I suddenly knew that I had to speak with you."

Intrigued, Dontae leaned forward. Put his elbows on the desk and asked, "Just tell me how I can help. Whatever you need, I'm here for you." *Unlike the time that I just wussed out on you.*

"Five years ago when I was in prison, a prison ministry team preached one Sunday. I didn't have anything else to do so I went and I listened." Stevie touched his heart as he continued. "I felt something that day, but I had so much anger built up in me that I rejected it. I remember praying in my seat while tears rolled down my face. I told the Lord that day, that if He could tell me why Linden picked me rather than you, then I would serve him."

Dontae felt some kind of way about Stevie's confession, because he had wasted so much time when all the while, this man had been waiting on an answer that only he or Coach Linden could have given him. But Dontae had been too busy avoiding the truth to be of help to anyone. Time to stop avoiding and just tell it like it was.

"He came after me first, Stevie. But I was so drunk and scared when he came into my room that I threw up all over myself. He had the audacity to leave my room looking as if he was disgusted by all the vomit on me and the floor."

Shaking his head, Stevie said, "I kept thinking that even though I knew that I liked women, I must be gay deep down or he never would have come at me like that."

"I wondered the same thing about myself. How a man could even approach another man like that... but a very smart and beautiful woman recently told me that I am not what was done to me. Linden didn't care what either one of us wanted. He is a selfish and sick man and that's why I have decided to testify against him. It's my way of apologizing for not being there for you that night."

"Look man, we were both drunk that night. I probably wouldn't have been able to help you either. All I remembered was going to that room and stripping down. Back then I always slept in the nude. But I haven't done that since that snake snuck in my room. Even with my wife, I have to put on my pajamas before I go to sleep."

"When I travel, and I'm in hotel rooms, I sleep with the television on. Just can't deal with the darkness like that when I'm in a strange place."

"I should testify, too. My family has always wondered what happened to all my potential. I think it's high time that I told them." Stevie looked as if three tons of steel had been lifted off of him. After ten years of torture, he was finally coming alive again.

"With both of us standing behind the other accuser, Linden won't be able to walk away from his crimes. He's going down."

"I'm trying not to wish for the worst of the worst for Linden, especially since I'm getting ready to call my wife and tell her that I'll be attending church with her this Sunday."

"I think I'll attend with my—" he almost called Jewel his fiancée but then he remembered that she'd given back the ring, "girlfriend."

"All right man." Stevie stood. "Don't be a stranger; I don't live far from Charlotte, so we're practically neighbors."

Dontae stood and walked around his desk. He hesitated for a second, but only a second. "What kind of work are you looking for?"

Stevie smiled, "I'm a jack of all trades. I do whatever puts the food on the table."

"I might have a job for you," Dontae said.

"Hey, I'm not looking for a handout. You don't owe me anything. I reached up and grabbed that room key and I drunk my own self into a stupor. It wasn't your fault, so you don't owe me anything."

"I'm not offering you a handout. I remember how good you used to be at spotting winners and losers. I'm looking for a scout to help me grow my business. Does that seem like something you'd be interested in?"

Stevie got excited. Then he caught himself, like someone who had been told over and over again not to expect anything good out of life. "You for real?"

"As real as real gets."

"I've been watching high school and colleges games for the longest, picking out the players that I thought could go the distance. I could do that job in my sleep." Stevie held out a hand to Dontae. "You got a deal, man. Thanks."

"See you on Monday," Dontae said, after giving him the location of his office. When Stevie walked out the door, Dontae sat down and exhaled... redemption sure felt good.

11

Ramsey had been praying for her, her children had been praying and Carmella had also spent much of her time in prayer, asking God why bad things happen to good people. She'd been tempted to just lie in bed for a month to protest this horrible thing that her family now had to endure. But Carmella had committed her life to God a long time ago, so she knew she couldn't continue moping around as if Jesus had come down from the cross and refused to die for the sins of the world.

Her son had been violated, that was a fact. But so many other things in Dontae's life were beautiful and blessed of God. Her son had been drafted into the NFL, and even though he'd hurt his knee the first year in, Dontae had still been able to keep his signing bonus, which enabled him to start his own business. Dontae was now a millionaire in his own right. If Carmella didn't know nothing else, she knew that God was in the work-it-out business. Some things might take a little longer to get worked out, but in God's good time, it would all be sorted out.

Like the problem Dontae was having with trusting God for a lifelong marriage. Carmella had prayed that Dontae would soon come to realize that love only lasts when two people are willing to work together, and defend their love against the whole world. Dontae was so stuck on how things had ended with her and Nelson that he had totally missed the fact that he was not his daddy and that through the power of Jesus Christ he could break the curse of divorce off of his life. She prayed that for Dontae and for the day that he would be able to remove from his memory even the thought of Coach Linden.

Since Carmella believed that God was a prayer-answering God, she forced herself to stop crying and to praise God even though things didn't turn out the way she'd expected. Sitting in front of her computer, Carmella turned on her radio. Fred Hammond was singing *Running Back to You*. She cranked it up as she began her first Praise Alert since Dontae's awful news.

As always, she began the alert, which went out to Ramsey and their seven children, with her favorite scripture in Psalm 150: *Praise ye the Lord. Praise God in His sanctuary: praise Him in the firmament of His power. Praise Him for His mighty acts: praise Him according to*

His excellent greatness. Let everything that hath breath praise the Lord. Praise ye the Lord.

Today she noticed something in those scriptures that she'd never paid much attention to before. The verse didn't say praise God because everything was wonderful in her life, or because God had answered all her prayers and she had need of nothing. No, this verse simply admonished her to praise God just because of who He is... and that's what she intended to do. "Thank you, Jesus," she whispered as her fingers danced in praise over her computer keys.

She began writing: I normally send out praise reports that other people have written. But today I want to share with you some things that have been on my heart. First off, my prayer is that none of you ever have to deal with anything in life that causes you to lose your ability to praise God. In my fifty-plus years on this earth, I have dealt with two issues that almost stole the praise from my lips: The divorce from my first husband and the molestation of my son. I couldn't understand how people in this world could be so evil and how things like this could happen. But these last few days I have spent most of my time studying the Bible. And as I was reading the twenty-fourth chapter of Matthew, it all became clear to me.

In the beginning of that chapter, one of the disciples asked Jesus to tell them what signs to look for so they could tell when the end of the world was near. The answer that Jesus gave sounded a lot like the world we are living in now. He said,

Ye shall hear of wars and rumors of wars: see that ye be not troubled: for all these things must come to pass, but the end is not yet. For nation shall rise against nation, and kingdom against kingdom: and there shall be famines, and pestilences, and earthquakes, and divers places. All these are the beginning of sorrows.

Then shall they deliver you up to be afflicted, and shall kill you: and ye shall be hated of all nations for my name's sake. And then shall many be offended, and shall betray one another, and shall hate one another. And many false prophets shall rise, and shall deceive many. And because iniquity shall abound, the love of many shall wax cold. But he that shall endure to the end, the same shall be saved.

And the gospel of the kingdom shall be preached in all the world for a witness unto all nations; and then shall the end come.

After writing those verses, Carmella grabbed a tissue and dabbed her eyes a few times. She then continued her email to her children...

I'm in tears as I am writing this to you all because I see it so clearly now. Evil is running rampant in this world because the devil knows his time is short... he knows that God is about to sound the trumpet and all those who have endured the hardships of this wicked generation and kept the faith will one day see the glory of God revealed. So

I'm asking all of you, the Marshalls and the Thomases, to keep the faith and never lose your praise.

As for me and Ramsey, we will always praise and thank the Lord for the seven beautiful children we now share. You all are so precious to us and we continually pray blessings over your lives, even knowing that the evil one will try to block your blessings. But be of good cheer, because the God Ramsey and I serve has overcome the world and the evil one. But Ramsey and I will not always be here to pray over you or to praise the Lord for you. These are things that every one of you must learn to do for yourselves.

So from this day forward, I am challenging each one of you to find your praise. I will email you praise reports from time to time, but I will also be looking for your individual praise reports. Time is short and no one knows when the end will be. But one thing I do know... I intend to make it to heaven, and I want to see all of you there with me.

And remember, if God never does anything else for you, He's already done enough.

***

Holding hands as they strolled down the streets of a strip mall, Dontae and Jewel seemed at ease with each other after a night of dinner and a movie. "I like this."

"Like what?" Jewel asked with a raised brow.

"Us... you and me." He stopped walking, turned to her and while gazing in her eyes, trying to communicate all the love he felt, he said. "I want us to be together, Jewel. I feel as if a part of me is missing, with the way things stand between us."

Jewel put her hand on Dontae's face as she told him as gently as possible, "And I want you to fight for our love."

That comment angered Dontae. He stepped away from her and lifted his hands heavenward as he tried to rein himself in. He'd been doing everything he knew to do for months now, trying to get back into her good graces. If that wasn't fighting for their love, then what was it? Turning back towards her, Dontae demanded, "What do you think I've been doing?"

"Oh, you've got a lot of fight in you right now." She crossed her arms and stared at him for a long moment. "But what about five, ten or even twenty years from now? What happens when we've been married so long that we can't even remember how it felt to be young and in love anymore... will you fight for our love then?"

Dontae really wanted to say yes to five years from now, yes to ten years from now and even yes to twenty years from this very day. But it was always in the back of his mind that his mother and father divorced after twenty-three years. His parents didn't have a prenup and therefore his father found himself being raked over hot coals in the divorce proceedings... not that he didn't deserve it, but dang.

They got back in the car. Dontae turned to her and said, "Real talk?"

Jewel nodded.

As they sat beside each other, in the parking lot of one of their favorite shopping centers, Dontae felt it was time to say what truly troubled him. "I love you with all my heart. But I don't know what the future holds. Who's to say that I won't turn out to be just like my father and decide that twenty years is enough with one woman and then want a divorce so I can marry someone else?"

"Real talk?" she asked of him.

It was Dontae's turn to nod.

"If you could do me like that after I spent all those years loving you and making a home for the family I hope to have with you... then you deserve to lose your money."

"You would take all of my money?" Dontae asked incredulously.

"If you could cheat on me and then trade me in for some teenager, I certainly would take all—" she paused, then corrected herself, "half your money. I think that's a fair price to pay for breaking my heart, don't you?"

Dontae didn't know what to say to that. Jewel hadn't gotten herself injured on the football field and she didn't go in to his office every day and bust her butt for his clients. He did all the work and he really didn't think it fair that he'd have to split the spoils if their marriage should come to an end. But he also knew that Jewel wasn't a gold digger. She wasn't looking for an easy paycheck. She truly believed that not having a prenup would make Dontae want to stay and work things out. Whether that was true or not, Dontae couldn't say.

He drove Jewel home, walked her to the door and when he tried to kiss her good night, she stopped him. "I think we first need to figure out what we are going to do before we cloud the issue any further."

Dontae nodded, then asked, "Do you still want me to pick you up for church in the morning?"

"I would like that very much," Jewel told him.
"Okay, well I'll be here at eight in the morning, so we can do breakfast before church." With that said, Jewel went into the house leaving Dontae standing on the porch looking lost and alone.

12

When Dontae arrived home Ramsey Jr. and Ronny wanted to know how he felt about the email his mother had sent out that night. Since he'd been busy pouring out his heart to Jewel, he hadn't seen the email yet. His brothers seemed to really want to get his feedback, so Dontae went to his room and turned on his computer. His mother hadn't sent them a Praise Alert in a few weeks, so even though Dontae wouldn't admit it to his brothers, he was kind of excited about reading what his mom had to say.

As he opened the email and read the first few paragraphs, Dontae didn't know whether he should be angry with his mother for putting his business out there or if he should feel sorry for how hard the knowledge of what happened to him hit her. He double checked the "sent to" area and was comforted by the fact that the email was only sent to their immediate family... since his brothers and sisters already knew the story, Dontae wasn't upset with his mother.

Even though he didn't like thinking about that horrible incident, he decided to continue reading to discover what else his mother had to say. He was totally caught off guard by the statement about the end times. But ever since he was a little boy, his mom had always talked about something called the rapture, when the people of God would suddenly disappear and then God would judge the ones that had been left behind. Dontae seriously doubted that the world was about to come to an end, but the more he read from the twenty-fourth chapter of Matthew that his mother had mentioned in her email, he began to wonder if she wasn't right. The world did seem a lot more evil these days, with people doing whatever they pleased no matter how it affected anyone else.

When he was a kid, Dontae used to trust in God and people in general. But things happened that destroyed his trust in mankind and those things had even rocked his faith. He'd never told his mom that his faith wasn't where it used to be, but somehow she had known. And now she was asking him to keep the faith that he'd laid down a long time ago. "How can I praise God when," Dontae poked his forehead with his index finger, "my head is still all messed up?" Dontae was talking to the computer screen as if his mom was on Skype or doing FaceTime with him and she could answer his questions.

Dontae's life had been affected by a man who thought he could use and abuse young boys and never face any consequences. Dontae had tried his best to move past the pain and humiliation that night caused him. But there was another man in his life who had caused him pain that had not been so easy to sweep under the rug. The way his father left his mother after claiming for years to be so in love with his wife, had stunned him.

To be honest Dontae wished that he could just open his mouth and praise the Lord for doing this or that for him. But right now things were so jacked up that he just wasn't going to be able to do that. He turned off his computer and even though he knew his brothers were waiting for him to come out of his room and discuss the email with them, he just couldn't face them right now either. So he turned off his laptop and went to bed hoping to drown out the cares of life.

But his troubles seemed to meet him in his sleep as tossed and turned, this way and that way, trying to figure out what was going on and why he couldn't seem to find anyone. His mother was gone, his brothers and sisters were gone. Dontae became frantic in his dream-like state of mind. He worried that something terrible might have happened to the people he loved and then his heart felt as if it was about to jump out of his body as Jewel's face appeared before him.

She said, "I tried to wait for you."

What did that mean? Had Jewel given up on him and found someone else? Not his Jewel. She wouldn't have left him like everyone else had. He rushed over to her house and pounded on the door. He pounded on that door until his fist started to bleed. "Open the door!" he screamed.

"She ain't there," Dontae heard someone behind him say.

He turned around and saw an unkempt bearded man. "Where is she?"

The man didn't say anything, just looked up and pointed heavenward.

"What do you mean?" Dontae mimicked the man by pointed heavenward. "I asked where is she... do you know or not?"

"They're all gone. My family, Jewel, and even old lady Maggie down the street. My wife kept warning me, but I wouldn't listen... I wouldn't listen," the man said again with much sorrow in his voice as he walked away from Dontae, looking as if he was heading nowhere in particular, just out roaming the earth.

Then other people came down the street looking as if they were aimlessly roaming the earth also, but they were all headed in the same direction. As Dontae stood there watching, hundreds, then thousands, then tens of thousands of zombie-like people walked past him. Curious, Dontae began following them.

The walk was long and hard. Several people got in fights. Dontae witnessed one stabbing after the next, but the zombie-like people would just get back up after bleeding out and start walking again. "Where are we going?" Dontae screamed. The world had gone mad, and he needed answers.

The next thing Dontae saw was his dad and Coach Linden in front of him. His dad took out a gun and Dontae shouted, "Don't do it, Dad. You'll just end up back in prison."

But Nelson didn't seem to care about prison or about the fact that it was broad daylight. He lifted his gun and unloaded it into Coach Linden's body. Dontae watched the man fall to the ground. Even though Dontae knew that Coach Linden had to be dead after being shot so many times, he was still tempted to kick the man. But as he approached, his dad reached out a hand to stop him.

"You're a better man than me, son. Let the Lord fight your battles, just like your mama taught you." After saying that Nelson drifted into the crowd. Then Coach Linden got back up and continued roaming the streets with the rest of the zombies.

Dontae was so confused by everything he was witnessing. All types of evil and degradation was going on. People were being murdered left and right, but none of them were able to stay dead. What in the world was going on?

All of a sudden everyone seemed to stop and lift their heads, staring into the sky as the heavens seemed to open up and a booming voice said, "*Why do you seek Me now? Why do you long for what you cannot have*?"

At those words the people around Dontae began weeping. Then they started clawing as if trying to reach the sky.

The booming voice said, "*Depart from me. I never knew you.*"

Suddenly Dontae realized who was speaking. It was God and Dontae didn't like the fact that he was being included in the same boat with all these zombies. Dontae lifted his eyes to the Lord and asked, "What about me, Lord? Don't you know me?"

"*I once knew you. But you refused to trust Me.*"

That's not fair, Dontae wanted to shout and scream at the Lord. Of course he didn't trust God... he didn't trust anyone. How could he be held accountable for that? "*Don't You know what happened to me?*"

God simply said, "*Don't you know who I am? I am the God who wanted to heal you. But you chose not to come to Me. And now I will not come to you.*"

"No!" Dontae reached out a hand, hoping and praying that he could stretch that hand long enough to reach heaven. But the heavens had closed up and darkness descended upon the earth. And everyone he loved was gone; he couldn't even find his father anymore, since he had taken off running after shooting Coach Linden. Dontae was alone, but he didn't want to be alone. He wanted to live, love and laugh. But his mom's words kept coming back to him... the end of days... the end of days.

Dontae turned from one side to the next, watching all of the horror and confusion that was unfolding right before his eyes. His mother had told him that after God pulled his chosen people out of the earth and the ones that had been left behind realized that there was no longer any hope for them—that they were doomed to die without Christ— the people would cry out to God, but would not be heard. He was witnessing that now. As the heavens had shut up to them and no one was able to get an answer from the Lord, the people's eyes grew hard with hatred and they began shaking their fists toward heaven.

But Dontae didn't blame God for his fate. As he stood there in the midst of the lost, knowing that he was one of them, he remembered his mother telling him that he didn't know God for himself, that he only knew about her God. And he realized that he needed to spend the rest of his life, no matter how miserable it would be, getting to know God for himself.

Tears drifted down Dontae's face as he got on his knees, steepled his hands and began praying to a God that wasn't interested in hearing from him anymore. But at that moment, Dontae had nowhere else to turn and since he knew that God was merciful, he figured he'd give it a shot.

But as he was praying, the angry mob all around him noticed and they didn't like what they saw. One of them hollered at Dontae, "Get up! Don't you know that prayer is for fools? There is no God."

Another proclaimed, "Can't you see all the destruction around us? Doesn't that tell you that God is just some mythical being? Stop wasting your time, get up and help us find the families we have lost."

But Dontae ignored them and just kept praying, telling God that he didn't want to live in a world without Him. That he would hold on to his faith and trust and believe that God would one day come back for him. As Dontae continued praying and continued to believe that he would one day be rejoined with his family, he felt a kick to his back and a blow to the head. He unsteepled his hands and opened his eyes, wondering what the devil was going on.

The mob had turned on him. From every which way he looked, people were picking up sticks and coming at him with knives. They were foaming at the mouth, as one blow and then another assaulted his body. Dontae tried to get up and run, but the assault was too brutal; he couldn't get away. He felt helpless, just as he had that night Coach Linden had entered his bedroom. But this time, instead of throwing up all over himself, he called on the name of the Lord to free him from the attack... and the funny thing was, now that God had left the earth to its own kind, Dontae actually trusted that God would and could deliver him.

***

"Wake up, man... wake up."

Why were they still pulling on him? Didn't they know that the Lord was coming for him? Maybe he needed to shout louder. "Jesus! Jesus!" Dontae was shouting at the top of his lungs, calling on the only help he could turn to. Because even though his father had been lost with him, and even though his father had finally slayed the animal who'd attacked him, that animal didn't stay dead and Dontae hadn't seen his earthly father since Linden had gotten back up and continued to roam the earth. But his heavenly Father was another story. Dontae now knew that he could always turn to Him for help.

"Wake up, bro. And stop hitting me before I hit you back."

That was Ronny's voice. His eyes popped open and he saw that Ramsey Jr. and Ronny were standing over him. "Y'all got left behind, too?"

"What?" Ramsey had this puzzled look on his face.

Then Dontae got a puzzled look on his face as he familiarized himself with his surroundings. "Am I in my bed?"

"Of course you're in your bed. Where did you think you were?" Ronny asked.

Dontae sat up, rubbed his eyes. He hadn't been left behind. It was all just a horrible nightmare. "Oh, thank God."

"Might we ask what you are thanking God for this morning? Maybe we can put it in a praise report and send it out to Mama Carmella," Ramsey said with a smirk of laughter on his face.

Ignoring the question, Dontae asked, "What time is it?"

"Almost nine in the morning," Ronny reported.

Suddenly Dontae remembered his promise to Jewel. They were supposed to do breakfast before church. He jumped out of bed. "I'm late. I've got to go." He jumped in the shower, threw on one of his suits that had already been to the cleaners and was nicely pressed. But before he ran out of the house, he pulled two things out of his top dresser drawer and put them in his jacket pocket.

By the time he got to Jewel's house it was too late, she had already left. He stood on her porch paralyzed for a moment, waiting to see if that bearded man would walk by and tell him that Jewel and a bunch of her neighbors had just disappeared. But no such man approached him, so he breathed a sigh of relief as he jumped back in his car and raced over to her church.

The praise and worship team was singing *How Great is our God*. It was an old worship song, but it did the trick. Dontae raised his hands and sang along, because after the horrible dream he'd endured the night before, he realized that God was great and mighty, even if He didn't do anything else for him... as long as He didn't leave him behind after the rapture, Dontae would praise Him. So, that's what he did, all through that worship song and the next. Dontae smiled at himself, wishing that his mom was there to see him, somehow he knew that she would be proud. Even though it took a nightmare to show him the way, Dontae finally realized that God was worthy to be praised, just because of who He is.

After praise and worship and the offering, the pastor stood behind the podium and read from John 16:32-33

Behold, the hour comes, yea, is now come, that ye shall be scattered, every man to his own, and shall leave me alone: and yet I am not alone, because the Father is with me. These things I have spoken unto you, that in me ye might have peace. In the world ye shall have tribulation: but be of good cheer; for I have overcome the world.

After hearing those verses, Dontae wasn't able to concentrate on anything else the pastor had to say, because it was as if God Himself had spoken those words to him. In his dream last night he had felt as if he was scattered, and tossed to and fro and so, so very alone. But even with all the things he'd witnessed in that horrible dream and in his own life, he still felt as if he could somehow reach God. Coach Linden trying to take advantage of him didn't matter anymore, Tory only wanting him for his money was a non-issue and his father leaving his family at a time when they needed him most didn't matter either—because God Himself would help Dontae overcome all of his tribulations.

By the time the altar call was made, Dontae was ready. He lifted his hands and walked down to receive Christ, *his* own personal savior. And as he was rejoicing, he turned and saw Jewel. Tears were flowing down her face and he could see the love of God all over her as he hadn't seen it before. This was the woman for him, not just today or tomorrow, but for the rest of his life. She was heaven sent, and he would never let her go.

He walked over to the woman that God had placed in his life to have and to hold forever and a day and he took the prenup out of his jacket pocket and tore it up. He then took the ring out of his pocket and held it out to her again as he said, "I don't need a prenup, Jewel. With God's help I promise you, I will fight for our marriage until the very end."

"That's all I wanted to hear," she said as she kissed him and then allowed Dontae Marshall to slide the ring back onto her finger, where it would stay as a symbol of their forever kind of love.

Epilogue

Six months later, Dontae testified against Coach Linden. He felt good about his part in helping to put a predator just where he belonged. But it was Stevie's testimony that really did Coach Linden in. Stevie was a new man and he and his family seemed to easily move beyond the pain of his past. Dontae decided is time for him to do the same. At the sentencing, when Dontae spoke, he looked Coach Linden directly in the eye and said, "After this day, you will most likely spend the rest of your days in prison, but I will not allow you to imprison me any longer. If I've learned anything from this experience, it's that I can't change the past and I don't have to dwell in it either. So, I will forget about you and move forward. I will have a happy life. What you do with the rest of yours is your business. But I pray that you allow God to work on your heart and to deliver you.

After that Dontae left the courtroom not even needing to hear just how many years Coach Linden received as his sentence. They were running late and a limo was outside the courthouse waiting for Dontae and Jewel. They had gotten married the week before and were now headed to the airport to begin their two week honeymoon in Paris and Italy. As far as Dontae was concerned, his bride deserved no less. She was a Godly woman who taught him to love, so he was about to show her some serious love in a place that was made for lovers.

But as they pulled up to the airport, Dontae remembered something he forgot to do. Now that they were at the airport, it would have to wait. He got out of the car and waited as the limo driver handed their bags over to the porter. He tipped the driver, grabbed his wife's hand, then rushed into the airport. After going through the check point and racing toward their terminal, they made it to the gate just as passengers were boarding the aircraft.

Dontae kissed Jewel as they sat down in their first class seats, but he kept reminding himself about what he forgot to do. He didn't have his laptop because he refused to take it on his honeymoon. But he did have his iPad. Dontae took it out of his carry-on bag and quickly opened his email. It was time for him to send his first Praise Alert.

Before typing his praise report, he added Jewel's email address to the circulation. She was now part of the family and should take part in their little praise-a-thon also. Dontae then began to type.

Hey Family, I'm on the plane getting ready to start my honeymoon, but I didn't want to leave the country before I sent out my very first Praise Alert. There was a time in my life when I didn't think I had anything to praise God for, but I now know differently. God has done so much for me; I hardly know where to begin. But I would first like to thank and praise God for the loving family that I have. You all have meant so much to me and I doubt I'd be where I am today without your support.

But the thing I am most thankful for is how God kept on blessing me even when I didn't deserve or appreciate Him for doing it. My mindset has totally changed and I can now praise God just for waking me up this morning, but not only that... I woke up next to the most beautiful woman in the world... sorry sisters, you all have to take a backseat to Jewel. But I think all of you are beautiful, too.

God has been good to me. I even thank and praise Him for allowing me to be able to give my wife the honeymoon of her dreams... isn't God good? He sure has been good to me. I will forever praise Him for leading and guiding me all of the days of my life, and for renewing my mind.

Now I have given you my praise report; I'm sure as time goes by I will have many more. But I'd like to hear from some of you. So whose next... what do you have to praise God for?

Dontae smiled as he wrote those words, because he knew his brothers and sisters loved God, but a few of them had lost their praise. Now was the perfect time to get it back.

The stewardess said, "Please turn off all electronic devices."

Well family, it's time for me to go, but before I sign off, I'd like to reiterate what Mom always tells us. No matter what trials or tribulations we go through in life, just go on and praise God anyhow.

The End

For info on other books in the series, join my mailing list:
http://vanessamiller.com/events/join-mailing-list/

Books in the Praise Him Anyhow series
Tears Fall at Night (Book 1 - Praise Him Anyhow Series)

Joy Comes in the Morning (Book 2 - Praise Him Anyhow Series)
A Forever Kind of Love (Book 3 - Praise Him Anyhow Series)
Ramsey's Praise (Book 4 - Praise Him Anyhow Series)
Escape to Love (Book 5 - Praise Him Anyhow Series)
Praise For Christmas (Book 6 - PHA Series)
His Love Walk (Book 7 - PHA Series)

Ramsey's Praise

Excerpt of Book 4 in the
Praise Him Anyhow Series

by

Vanessa Miller

1

She was standing about six feet away from him, holding a beautiful bridal bouquet when Ramsey Thomas first took notice of her. Long flowing hair, olive skin tone, sparkling hazel colored eyes. The gown she wore showed off every bit of her shapely body. Ramsey was almost to the point of drooling when his brother Ronny nudged his shoulder and said, "Please tell me you're not drooling over the bride like that?"

Ramsey turned to his brother with furrowed eyebrows. The bride was Jewel Dawson and she was marrying his younger brother, Dontae Marshall. Ramsey was the best man so it would be a bit awkward if he was standing before God and a whole congregation of folks, lusting after the bride. "Shut up, idiot. I'm not drooling over Jewel," Ramsey whispered and then turned back around so he could continue taking in the lovely view of Maxine Dawson, Jewel's oldest sister and maid of honor.

A few months back Dontae had tried to hook him up with one of the Dawson sisters, but he'd been completely wrong about which one Ramsey would be interested in. Dawn, the middle sister, although just as beautiful as her other sisters, she was too short for him, and their personalities leaned more toward them becoming best of friends rather than having any kind of love connection. But Maxine Dawson was a woman that Ramsey would like to invest some time getting to know.

As if feeling his gaze on her, Maxine's eyes met Ramsey's just as the preacher said, "I now pronounce you man and wife." As Dontae took Jewel in his arms, Ramsey winked at Maxine. He grinned as her cheeks turned red from blushing.

Ramsey wanted to ask her on a date right then and there. But no matter how much Maxine was taking up space in his head, he wouldn't do anything to spoil this moment for his brother.

Later that evening while at the reception, Ramsey was standing with his father, Ramsey senior and his stepmother, Carmella when they started in on him. "I guess we'll be attending your wedding next, eh, son?"

Ramsey ignored his father and let his eyes span the room. He was looking for Maxine, but he'd never admit that to his father, and certainly not to Mama Carmella. If she knew he had his eye on a woman, she'd start praying and call down Elijah, Moses and a couple heavenly angels to get Ram to make a move. Ram was the nickname Carmella had given him. His family had taken to calling him that as a way of distinguishing between him and his father.

"Who's Renee talking to?" Carmella asked, pointing over by some tables in the back.

Ramsey's head swiveled back around. He had three sisters, Joy, Raven and Renee. And he was very protective of all of them. But he tended to watch out for Renee just a bit more. The girl made a career out of finding bad in a room full of good. Ramsey recognized the smooth talker Renee was grinning up at immediately. Marlin Jones was a high powered real-estate developer whom Ramsey had dealt with on occasion. He didn't like the way the man did business. There was something too slick about him. "I'll be back," Ramsey told his parents.

Carmella caught his arm. "Now Ram, don't you go over there bothering your sister. She is old enough to make her own decisions."

"I'm not going to do anything. I know the guy, so I just want to say hello." And goodbye, he added under his breath. As Ram pressed forward, Marlin put his hand on Renee's shoulder, her head fell back as she laughed ridiculously at something the man said. Marlin must have been telling Renee the funny one about how his tax returns were complete fiction and how the IRS was about to audit him for all of his wrongdoing.

"I like the way you laugh. I normally don't come to weddings, but I'm so glad I accepted this invitation," Marlin was saying as Ram advanced on them.

"And why is that?" Renee asked, beaming up at Marlin.

"Because I met the most beautiful girl in the whole state of North Carolina."

Ram wanted to throw up all over Marlin's playa rap. He only prayed that Renee could see through him. But just in case she couldn't, he was about to do some playa hating. Ram tapped Marlin on the shoulder, getting his attention. "Marlin, I didn't know you were attending my brother's wedding."

Swinging around, Marlin had to lift his head to address Ramsey, who was at least a half foot taller than he. "Hey Ramsey, I had no idea that Dontae was your brother. But my mom is best friends with Jewel's mom, so I had to come."

"Gotcha." Ramsey threw a look at Renee and then told Marlin, "Well it was nice seeing you. Do you mind if I have a word with my little sister?"

"I thought Charlotte was a big city. But look how small it's suddenly become. I cannot believe that this beautiful woman standing next to me is related to someone with a mug like yours," Marlin said lightheartedly.

"Believe it." Ram didn't know how much longer he could hold his fake smile in place, so he quickly put his arm around Renee and began walking away from Marlin. "See you later," Ram said while still smiling and waving.

"What are you up to, Ram?"

"I'm just trying to get you away from that guy."

With a quizzical expression on her face, Renee wanted to know, "Why in the world would you do something like that?" She pointed toward Marlin. "The guy is a dream...

successful, handsome. There's no bum stamp on his forehead."

"Yeah, but there ought to be a dog stamp on it," Ram replied back.

Rolling her eyes, Renee shoved her brother. "Don't start this stuff tonight, Ram. Just go back to the head table with the rest of the bridal party and stay out of my business."

Ram opened his mouth to protest, but Renee lifted her index finger and pointed toward his table. "Go, Ram. I'm not going to let you ruin my fun tonight."

He tried to help her. But if his sister wanted to be foolish and fall all over herself for a man who might be in prison in the next year or so, then she could have all the temporary fun she wanted. Ram turned toward the head table and saw Maxine seated next to his chair, eating a piece of wedding cake. So he took his sister's advice and set about minding his own business. He grabbed a piece of cake off the cake table and then took his seat. "Is this cake as good as you are making it look?"

Maxine picked up her napkin and wiped her mouth. "Did I look like I was starving?"

"You were getting it in, that's for sure."

"I deprived myself of all sweets for over a decade. Now that I don't have to worry about being rail thin anymore, I was probably a little too excited about eating this cake."

Ramsey picked up his napkin and wiped the white icing she'd missed from her chin. "Don't worry about it, cake looks good on you."

"I bet you say that to all the girls," Maxine joked as she took another bite of her cake.

Ramsey thought about the line he'd just heard Marlin running on his sister and he didn't want to come across like that. But if he was honest with himself, from the moment he saw her, he'd been mesmerized. He wanted to get to know this woman in the worst way and he wasn't trying to blow his opportunity by acting like a jerk. "I'm not trying to hand you a line. The plain truth is, I think you're beautiful and I would love to take you out some time."

Dontae, the groom and Ronny, the all around clown were standing behind them. Ramsey hadn't seen them until it was too late. After he told Maxine that he wanted to take her out, both Dontae and Ronny cupped their hand around their ear and said, "Say what?"

Okay, yeah, when Ramsey first came to the city and Dontae tried to hook him up with one of the Dawson sisters, he'd been adamantly against it. He hadn't wanted to be fixed up because he'd just gotten out of an awful relationship with a bipolar woman who made Glenn Close seem like a reasonable woman. So, he needed that hiatus. He turned to his brothers and said, "I'm gon' tell y'all like Renee just told me, get somewhere and mind your own business."

Ronny held his hands up. "We know when we're not wanted. And besides, we have better things to do than to watch you get shot down."

As his brothers walked off, Ramsey turned back to Maxine. "Excuse them. They don't know much about home training, outside training or any other kind of training, for that matter." A giggle escaped Maxine's beautiful lips. Ramsey saw an opening and took his shot. "See, I'm already making you laugh. Imagine how much fun the two of us would have on a date."

"I'm sure it would be wonderful." Maxine couldn't stop grinning. "It's just too bad that you didn't ask me out before I decided to become a mom."

Ramsey's eyes trailed downward and stopped at her mid-section. "I would have never guessed that you were pregnant. When are you due?"

"I'm not pregnant," she said matter-of-factly.

Ramsey took a bite of his cake, took a moment to chew it and then said, "Correct me if I'm wrong, but don't you need to be pregnant in order to become a mom?"

"I would love to have a husband before I become pregnant." Maxine shrugged. "But since my husband hasn't found me yet, I decided to adopt."

"A little impatient, aren't you?"

A tinge of regret dimmed Maxine's eyes as she said, "The truth is, I thought that I wanted nothing more than to be a model and once my modeling career was over, I intended to parlay that success into an acting career." She shrugged again. "But I can't act, I'm tired of modeling and since my biological clock is ticking like a time bomb, I decided to adopt."

Ramsey was a bit surprised that Maxine had shared so much with him, given the fact they didn't know each other well, but maybe she thought of him more like a brother, since her sister had just married his brother. He hoped to God that she didn't think of him that way, because he sure wasn't seeing a relative when he looked at her. "You look so young. I'm sure you have plenty of time to wait for the right man to come along."

"Like they say, black don't crack," Maxine told him with a smile. "But seriously, I'll be thirty-four next year, so I don't have very many baby-making years left."

Ramsey shook his head at that news.

"What?" Maxine asked.

"It's nothing. I'm just amazed that a woman as beautiful as you hasn't found a man willing to make a baby with you."

"It's more difficult than you think. Most of the men I date are either insecure about my success or they think I'm too controlling."

"I don't know what kind of men you've been dating, but I don't mind releasing a little control every now and then. And I think your brand of success is very attractive."

That caught her off guard. She couldn't think of a quick comeback, so she simply thanked him for the compliment.

"Now, about that date..."

"You are kind of cute. And I bet we'd really enjoy ourselves on a date. But I've already signed up for diaper duty. Sorry." With that said, Maxine got up and walked away from Ramsey.

Ronny walked back over to the table, leaned over to his brother and said, "Struck out, huh? Should have asked me or Dontae. We could have told you that those Dawson sisters ain't no easy win."

***

Ramsey was so tired when he arrived home that all he'd managed to do before falling into bed on top of his covers was take his jacket and tie off. Hearing Maxine talk about wanting to become a mother and being willing to adopt to make that happen, caused Ramsey to think about another woman who couldn't get rid of her child fast enough. He'd tried for over a year to get Brandi out of his head, but on a night like this his subconscious couldn't help but drag him kicking and screaming into that nightmare again.

Brandi was in his face yelling at him. Tears were rolling down her face as she kept demanding that he tell her why they couldn't work things out and be a family. Ramsey wanted to yell right back at her, "Because you're crazy." But she had torched his best suits the last time he'd informed her of the obvious. So he tried to reason with crazy, which was also probably a bad idea.

"Look Brandi, we gave it a go. But we aren't right for each other. You know that."

"Then what am I supposed to do with this?" Lightning fast, Brandi reached into her shirt and pulled out a baby. She was holding the child as if it was nothing more than a rag doll.

"Where'd you get that baby?" Ramsey was frantic, wondering who in their right mind would allow Brandi to watch their baby.

"She's ours, Ramsey. Our love child."

"Love didn't have nothing to do with it. And we do not have a baby."

The next thing Ramsey knew, he and Brandi were standing on the rooftop of his New York apartment and Brandi was holding the baby by its leg and threatening to throw it off the roof. "If you don't want me, then you don't deserve our child," she screamed.

"What are you doing, Brandi. Put that baby down."

"Say you love me, Ramsey. Say it!" The baby started crying.

Ramsey took a step toward Brandi. "You don't want to hurt that baby. Give her to me." He held out his hands.

Brandi stepped back; losing her footing, she began wobbling. Ramsey rushed over and helped to steady her. He then all but begged her to hand him the baby.

Brandi shook her head and ran away from him. "You'll never see this child again," she said just before jumping off the roof.

Screaming, Ramsey woke up in a cold sweat. Putting his hands to his face, Ramsey sat Indian style, trying to sort out what had just happened to him. "Lord, why can't I get that woman out of my head?"

***

In another bedroom, about three hours away from Ramsey, Carmella Marshall was on her knees giving praise to God. He had done so much for her and seen her family through so many trials that Carmella didn't know what else to do but be grateful. Carmella was well aware that as long as they kept on living, somebody in her family was going to go through something that might just bring tears to her eyes, but she chose to praise God anyhow. Like the bible says, weeping may endure for a night, but Carmella had discovered that joy, does indeed, come in the morning.

Her children from her first marriage, Joy and Dontae had discovered the joy in praising the Lord along the road of recovering from their parents' crumbling marriage. And now Carmella had her sights set on Ramsey, Jr. He was the oldest of the seven grown children that she and her current husband were proud to be parents of. But Ram was dealing with something that he hadn't yet turned over to the Lord. So, once Carmella finished giving praise to her Savior, she turned her son over to the only One who could help him. "Lord, You see all and You know it all. Something is bothering Ram and he won't talk to me or his father about it. But I'm asking You to fix it for him. Give him peace and teach him how to lean on You. Amen and in Jesus' name I pray this prayer, believing that it is already done, so I give You praise for Your wondrous works."

"Amen," Ramsey, Sr. spoke up in agreement with his wife. He lifted the covers. "Now come to bed so we can get some sleep."

Carmella smiled at her sleepy husband and climbed into bed next to him. She had no problems falling to sleep that night because she knew that somewhere past the clouds in the sky, God had received her prayer and He was already working things out for Ram. She couldn't wait to shout the victory and do a praise dance over what God was about to do in Ram's life. She decided that she wouldn't wait, she was going to dance all up and down the church aisle on Sunday. Carmella wasn't one of those Christians who needed to see the promise before she believed. "Whew. I praise You, Lord. Thank You for always blowing my mind with just how well You take care of us," she shouted through the room, before turning onto her side and falling to sleep.

About the Author

Vanessa Miller is a best-selling author, playwright, and motivational speaker. She started writing as a child, spending countless hours either reading or writing poetry, short stories, stage plays and novels. Vanessa's creative endeavors took on new meaning in1994 when she became a Christian. Since then, her writing has been centered on themes of redemption, often focusing on characters facing multi-dimensional struggles.

Vanessa's novels have received rave reviews, with several appearing on *Essence Magazine's* Bestseller's List. Miller's work has receiving numerous awards, including "Best Christian Fiction Mahogany Award" and the "Red Rose Award for Excellence in Christian Fiction." Miller graduated from Capital University with a degree in Organizational Communication. She is an ordained minister in her church, explaining, "God has called me to minister to readers and to help them rediscover their place with the Lord."

Vanessa has recently completed the For Your Love series for Kimani Romance and How Sweet the Sound for Abingdon Press, first book in a historical set in the Gospel era which releases March 2014. Vanessa is currently working on an ebook series of novellas in the Praise Him Anyhow series. She is also working on the My Soul to Keep series for Whitaker House.

Vanessa Miller's website address is: www.vanessamiller.com But you can also stay in touch with Vanessa by joining her mailing list @ http://vanessamiller.com/events/join-mailing-list/ Vanessa can also be reached at these other sites as well:

Join me on Facebook: https://www.facebook.com/groups/77899021863/
Join me on Twitter: https://www.twitter.com/vanessamiller01
Vie my info on Amazon: https://www.amazon.com/author/vanessamiller

CPSIA information can be obtained at www.ICGtesting.com
Printed in the USA
LVOW06s2133260715

447744LV00008B/56/P